"THE MERLIN SUBSIDIARY is packed with adversity and joy. This novella about friendship draws us into the world of ballroom dancing. Five middle-aged women, Elizabeth, Edith, Joan, Frances, and Cecilia, meet at the Merlin Dance Studio and form a club they name the Merlin Subsidiary. For them, dance becomes symbolic of courage, acceptance, adventure, reawakening, and unselfconsciousness. They use these newfound strengths to solve life's problems. They are forward looking and don't dwell on past issues because they agree 'it's how things turn out that matters.' Author Barbara Kussow offers us insight into ways to enrich our lives through dance—with, maybe even, a bit of 'Merlin's magic' thrown in!"

- Joan Wiley, Ph.D., ballroom dancer and author of "Thank you for the Dance."

THE MERLIN SUBSIDIARY

Stories & Poems

Barbara Kussow

Marie Sheets Publishing

ISBN: 978-1-7376076-4-9

For my daughter, Natalie Schneider Nelson, and my mother, Mary Elizabeth Nichols. They would have been proud.

ACKNOWLEDGMENTS

My gratitude to James Kussow and Laura Moorman
for their help in bringing this collection to fruition
and to Richard Schwartz for his cover work.

CONTENTS

"The only way to make sense out of change is to plunge into it, move with it, and join the dance."

— Alan Wilson Watts

STORIES

The Merlin Subsidiary

A Novella

CHAPTER 1

The Subsidiary

"Okay, let's just relax and be ourselves tonight," Elizabeth said, sensing the air of nervousness among her friends.

"Oh—and does that mean we can gossip and make fun of the guys we dance with at the studio—like we always do?"

"Now, Fran, behave yourself," Elizabeth scolded.

"We don't want to offend Cecilia," Edith chimed in. "She might not want to come again."

"Well, I'm just going to be me—let the chips fall where they may," retorted Frances.

But the others knew Frances, or Fran, as they usually called her, would rein in her sarcastic tendencies just a tad.

They had gotten comfortable as a foursome—friends who were a little like sisters who regarded each other with affection but with rivalries and frictions from personality differences.

Tonight, there was some anxiety because a new person was joining their group.

They would say, "Welcome. We're so glad you could join us." They would smile broadly as they helped Cecilia Wang off with her coat and swoon over the aroma of her offering to their potluck. But then what?

Cecilia Wang was an Asian woman about whom they knew little, except she, like them, liked to dance, the interest that had brought them together.

Elizabeth, who they all considered the nicest—Frances said she took "nice pills"—was the one to suggest that they invite Cecilia. The others agreed although privately they may have felt some reluctance—not from snobbishness but from mild anxiety about cultural differences.

"For all you know, she may have been born here and be as American as the rest of us. We'll find out when we get to know her," Elizabeth had told the group. Elizabeth was somewhat defensive about heritage. She always said she was small town USA, and beyond that, she knew nothing of her genealogy. Her deceased husband, Jim, a journalist and egalitarian, had always been disdainful of people who defined themselves too much through their genealogical heritage— although he had known that he had an Irish grandmother and a Jewish grandfather. She supposed that some of his attitude had rubbed off on her.

Edith, who proudly traced her heritage back to the Mayflower pilgrims, had offered to help members of the group with genealogy searches if they wanted to find out more about their family origins, but, thus far, no one had taken her up on the offer. Edith had a regal bearing and sometimes came across as holding feelings of superiority.

Frances referred to Edith as "the aristocrat" behind her back because Edith, along with her genealogical credentials, was the widow of a prominent doctor and had once described herself as having been an "excellent hostess" of dinner parties, presumably to movers and shakers of the city.

Frances said that her French grandmother had met her grandfather, an American soldier, when the Americans liberated France in World War II. Her mother, she said, was a descendant of Marie Antoinette, symbol of monarchical excesses, who may or may not have said of commoners, "Let them eat cake!" If the others doubted these aristocratic origins, they just smiled to themselves. Frances kept things interesting with her questionable stories and sometimes humorous or shocking statements. She probably concocted the story for one-upmanship over Edith.

"Cecilia is an English name, isn't it? How does a Chinese woman get named Cecilia?" asked Frances.

"Probably of Latin origin. Cecilia is a saint—maybe that has something to do with it," said Joan who is a lapsed Catholic. "She is patroness of music and important to the music of the liturgy of the Catholic Church. She is a martyr. There is a church in Rome named for her—and, of course, some churches in the U.S., too. I remember studying about her when I was young. She took a vow of chastity, but her parents insisted she marry a nobleman."

"You mean she was a martyr because she was forced to give up her virginity?" asked Edith, who mugs her incredulity. Edith is Methodist, reared by a mother who was antagonistic toward Catholicism.

"Um, no-oh, I don't think so. I don't remember why she was a martyr."

The doorbell rang.

"Maybe Cecilia will tell us about her name some time—but don't ask tonight—okay? Might come across as rude." Elizabeth spoke over her shoulder as she hurried to answer the door.

"So much for just being ourselves!" Frances rolled her eyes.

They called their informal social group the Merlin Subsidiary.

Proposed by Joan, the name was ironic, the reason for its appeal. It sounded corporate and official. They were quite the opposite—casual, social, and friendly.

They had come together through the Merlin Dance Studio near Cleveland, Ohio, where they attended dance parties and took group lessons. Each of them was single. Edith, Joan, and Elizabeth were widows, Frances divorced.

The group wasn't sure whether Cecilia, the newcomer, was divorced or still married. When she first started coming to the studio, she came with her husband, a man who looked morose and danced woodenly. It was apparent that he didn't enjoy dancing as much as Cecilia did. Then, she started to attend Saturday night dances by herself. Her husband didn't mind, she'd told Vera Moore, the owner of the studio. He was a college professor who liked to work on his research, and it was okay with him if she wanted to go dancing by herself. So, that was the grapevine version of the relationship, but after a while, people began to wonder if they had separated.

They ranged in age from 43 (Cecilia) to 58 (Edith and Joan). The Merlin Studio had a reputation for welcoming older singles. Vera Moore was herself a fiftyish woman (actual age carefully concealed), who got to know her clientele personally. She asked after their children, congratulated them on their achievements, and sympathized with their losses and disappointments.

The studio was low-budget, somewhat deteriorated, because it was housed in an aged building. At the entrance, there was a faded, black canopy, like you sometimes saw in nightclubs in movies, especially older movies, where there was a door attendant dressed in a uniform. But, of course, there was no uniformed doorman. To enter, dancers climbed a small flight of creaky stairs. Inside, its décor had touches that gave it glitz and glamour—a ceiling glitter ball, Chinese lanterns, miniature silvery white lights on branches stuck in large vases, a mirror-lined wall, and enlarged photos of smiling dancers dressed for exhibition. People liked its retro aura.

The studio wasn't large enough to accommodate larger tables for groups. There were chairs along the sides of the dance floor with a few small tables between seats for holding drinks and personal items. The wooden dance floor was small or medium, depending on who you asked, and well maintained. Vera wanted everyone to wear dance shoes, or at least, shoes that would not damage the floor. A dusty, old piano, badly in need of tuning, sat in one corner at the end of the floor. It was wheeled out at the Christmas dance for Vera to play while everyone gathered around it and sang carols and traditional holiday songs.

Women felt safe at the Merlin. Drinking and smoking were not allowed. Free coffee was always brewing, and a plate of finger foods was usually on a table at the end of the dance floor. The only time women might feel anxious was when they walked to their cars after the evening dance party. The solution was to pair up or ask one of the guys to walk with them. Occasionally a guy would press his attentions on a woman a little too aggressively, but Vera took care of the situation with a few carefully chosen words.

Frances, an out-of-towner who moved from Cincinnati, was the first of the group to discover the Merlin. Then came Elizabeth. Next, Joan and Edith came together. The two had met in a support group for parents of adult children with mental problems. The last to come was Cecilia.

CHAPTER 2

Kentucky Rebel

Frances grew up in the mountains of Kentucky. Her father was a coal miner, her mother a housewife until she had to go to work as a waitress to help support the family—Frances and four brothers. Frances was the oldest and often in charge of her brothers, who ranged from two to six years younger than she. By age seven, she was often left alone to care for Bobby, who was five. By age twelve, she was taking care of all of them, while her mother was at work. She was often a school truant, but her parents did not care. If her father was home, he was usually moody, sometimes half-drunk, and took no responsibility for the boys. They knew to stay out of his way and took to outdoor pleasures, exploring the woods, wading in the creek, and playing on a rickety, swinging pedestrian bridge.

On Saturday nights, her maternal grandmother would sometimes come and stay, and Frances was allowed to go to a barn dance with her parents. The barn dance was not really in a barn, but in a music hall that was part of a tavern. She loved to dance and looked forward to these nights. When she was young, she would dance with other girls and sometimes her mother and, occasionally, her father. He was a good dancer and when he whirled her around the floor, she forgave him for some of his many faults. At 13, she was tall enough to take part in square dancing. She loved the rules, the structure, the times when the men seemed more gallant and the women smiled more, flouncing their wide skirts. Her granny, the most supportive adult in her life, made her a wide skirt with stiff petticoats.

When her father got laid off from the coal mine, he became more and more quarrelsome and often ruined their Saturday nights. He got in fights, often accusing her mother of flirting with other men, or other men of flirting with her. At home, he was sometimes abusive. Her mother began to have bruises on her arm and neck and wore long sleeves and high collars to cover them.

Frances developed a crush on one of the guitar players in the band. Sometimes, she went to the stage and whispered a request for a song. It was a pretense to talk to him. He was in his mid-twenties, and, at first, paid little attention to her. Then, he became aware of her moony adoration and began to pay more attention. She didn't see the calculation behind his rakish smile. One night, her mother refused to go to the dance, and Frances went with her father, who danced with her once, then went outside to smoke and drink and swap stories with his friends. When intermission came for the band, the guitar player, Ted was his name, asked Frances to go outside and "get a breath of fresh air." In the "fresh air," he smoked and made minimal conversation, then said, "I've got to get something in my car. Want to come with me?" She went, and he grabbed her arm and pushed her down into the back seat. She said, "Please, no, I haven't ever done this…" But he put his hand over her mouth and began to remove her undies. She started to cry, and he pushed his hand harder on her mouth. "Shuddup! This is what you've been wanting, ain't it?" The stiff petticoat hindered him, and he swore and ripped it. And Frances cried out in pain as he pushed his way into her.

At 13, Frances had lost her virginity in a brutal way, and Ted went back into the music hall and played the second set of the evening. She staggered to her father's truck and huddled in the seat crying until she fell asleep. It was after midnight when her father climbed into the driver's seat. On the road, he nearly fell asleep at the wheel. Frances jumped, and he growled at her. "Yer goin' to make me have a wreck doin' that." A few minutes later, he stopped the truck, got outside, and vomited into the ditch.

At home the next day, Frances tried to get the blood off the petticoat, then to mend it. She didn't have her grandmother's seamstress skills, and the skirt was basically ruined. Anyway, she didn't want to wear it anymore. She hid it at the bottom of a box in their creaky attic.

A month or so later, she went to town with her mother to get groceries. After getting groceries, they went to the greasy spoon where her mom worked. While her mom was in the back talking to the manager, Frances waited in the booth, drinking a Coke. Then, she saw Ted come in with a brassy blond woman, made up with ruby red lipstick and heavy rouge, and wearing a tight skirt with stiletto heels. He had his arm around her possessively. Frances huddled in the booth, hoping he wouldn't see her. They walked past her on the way to another booth, and, for a second, he gazed at her but then looked away, as though he didn't recognize her. Later, she heard that the woman was his fiancée.

Frances managed to get through her freshman and sophomore years of high school with mostly C's and D's. She had native intelligence but was at a disadvantage because of poor attendance during grade school. She also found it difficult to study in their small, cramped cabin.

She quit high school when she was sixteen and went to work as a waitress. Her parents demanded that she give them money for "rent" for the tiny space in the attic she had claimed for herself. It was not bad in the spring and summer but was freezing in the winter. She often ended up sleeping on a pallet near their wood stove in the winter.

One night her father came home drunk. She woke up to find him squeezing her breasts and trying to stick his tongue in her mouth. She reacted instinctively, punching and kicking him. The commotion woke her mother, and he swore and scrambled away.

At dawn, Frances packed her meager belongings and left. She walked three miles to her grandparents' house, located on the outskirts of the town where she had attended high school and now worked.

Frances's mother said she was "making up stuff." Her father denied doing anything wrong. He said he'd had too much to drink and was showing fatherly affection. That was all it was. But gran believed otherwise. She stood up to Frances's parents and said she was old enough to make her own decisions now. Frances should come live with her and help take care of gramps. He was getting forgetful, and she was afraid he might burn the house down. She cleared out a storage room in their small house, and Frances had a tiny room all to herself with a cot, a dresser, and hooks to hang her clothes on. Frances luxuriated in the privacy and the warmth.

As far as Frances could tell, gramps was not particularly forgetful. That was just something gran told her mother to get her to leave Frances alone. Both grandparents were great storytellers. Evenings, they would entertain her with humorous stories about mountain people, and Frances began to tell her own stories. She surprised herself with a sense of humor, making gramps and gran laugh at her shrewd observations about townspeople.

After she'd been there about six months, gramps collapsed while taking a walk and died of a heart attack. Not long after that, it became apparent that gran was ill. For as long as Frances could remember, she had smoked a pipe, and now she had lung cancer. There was no treatment for it. She refused to go to hospice like a doctor recommended. Frances took care of her as best she could for the last three months of her life. Just before she died, she asked Frances to look in the back of a cabinet and find a box where she kept "special things." From it, she took a dingy envelope and held it out to Frances. "This is fer you, luv. Take it and git out of this place and make a better life fer yerself. Don't worry about yer ma. She'll get the house. Don't tell her about this money. She'll want it." There was nearly $500 in the envelope.

Frances grieved for the only person who she felt truly cared for her, but she was grateful that her granny had freed her. She found out that there was a Greyhound bus stop in a town 20 miles away. She left without telling her family. She started walking but, after several miles, she was fortunate enough to hitch a ride with an elderly couple.

She ended up in Cincinnati, Ohio, just across the Ohio River from Kentucky.

There, she found another waitress job in a good restaurant and a room in a boarding house where she shared a bathroom with three other single women. The landlady, Miss Sadie Brown, was kind enough, and she reminded her a bit of her gran, though a rung or two above her on the social ladder. She liked to give the women advice, and one day, she asked Frances if she had a high school diploma. No, she did not.

"Well, dear, you know, don't you that you can get it by studying by yourself. You can earn what is called a GED, get a better job. Go to the library and ask them. They'll tell you what you need to do. A GED will help you get a better job."

Frances took her advice, earned her GED, and followed it up by taking business courses at a community college.

Her hard scrabble life and its psychological injuries had left her with a brittle armor. She was defensive and often suspicious of people's motives. She'd dyed her red hair black so she wouldn't stand out as much. It might help prevent recognition, should her father come searching for her. She had a curvy figure and was quite attractive, but scarred by the rape and her father's behavior, she refused men's overtures.

Until she met Roy. Frances had been fortunate enough to get a job as a receptionist in a medical center. Roy was a pharmaceutical salesman, who liked to joke around. He was not the handsomest guy she'd ever met, but he had what the nurses called a "good personality." The first time he asked Frances out, she declined. He smiled and said, "Well, you're missing out on a wonderful experience. I'll ask again next time I come in."

He asked, and she accepted. He seemed to have plenty of money and took her to nice restaurants, dances, and the theatre. Like her father, he was a good dancer, and maybe that was why she finally agreed to marry him.

Six months after they married, he wanted her to quit her job and travel with him, as his sales route covered several eastern states. He promised they'd go to New York City to see the Empire State Building and Radio City Music Hall, among other places. They were carefree and had plenty of time to play after his sales calls. Most of their nights were spent in drinking, partying, and dancing in nightclubs or playing pinball and shooting pool in taverns.

Then, she got pregnant and felt tired and sick in the morning. One morning when they sat in a café, Frances was unable to eat. Roy leaned toward her and said, "Look, Fran, we got a good life... I don't know whether I'm cut out to be a dad... It's still early enough, you know. I know a doctor who would help us out..."

At first, Frances didn't know what he meant, but then, she looked at him and saw that he had a serious, vacant look, and, suddenly, she understood.

"You mean an abortion?"

"Well, yeah, lots of women do it. In my line of work, I got connections..."

Frances thought about her brothers—how she wanted to get away from the responsibility but also how she missed them sometimes. She knew her mother hadn't wanted Sammy, her youngest brother. She'd heard her yell at her father, "Men don't know how it is!" And he said something about how she had help. Fran was good with the boys. Fran would help. Yes, and Fran did help. Sammy called her "Fan," and liked to snuggle up to her. She decided she didn't want an abortion.

A doctor told Frances she should avoid alcohol while pregnant, and she no longer enjoyed going out with Roy at night. He went by himself, often coming home in the early morning hours.

Seven months into her pregnancy, Frances noticed that it had been three days since she felt the baby move. The doctor told her that she had suffered a stillbirth. She underwent induced labor to remove the baby from her womb.

Afterward, Frances felt emotionally drained, and depressed. Roy seemed relieved and, after a week or two, expected her to continue their partying. She tried but felt so out of it that she stopped going with him. They had little to say to each other, and after some time, she found out that he had visited prostitutes. She walked out and went back to Cincinnati, where she got her old job back because she had been a good worker. Roy filed for divorce, citing desertion so he wouldn't have to pay alimony, and she didn't contest it.

One evening, Frances went out for a stroll with woman named Betty from her boarding house. Her friend suggested they walk to a dance pavilion and watch the dancers. At first, Frances thought she didn't want to go. Her memories of dancing were a mixture of good and bad. She had loved dancing at country barn dances, but she was also assaulted there. Some of the best times with Roy had been when he took her dancing, but now, well—

She didn't reveal any of these thoughts to her companion, and so they walked to the pavilion. The floor was teeming with couples. Most of them seemed in their thirties or forties, but some were older, some younger, dancing to recorded music played by a disc jockey. Soon, her toes were tapping and her body swaying. She longed to be on the floor with them.

Betty watched her with amusement, "You're a good dancer, aren't you? I can tell."

Frances shrugged. "We could pay and go in, but I don't see any single men who would dance with us."

The following Saturday evening, they went to the pavilion again just to watch. Frances loved watching the dancers. She thought about how, even though they were dancing to the same music, they all had unique styles. Then, she scanned some of the people who were sitting at tables talking and nursing their drinks. They seemed to be spectators, as she and Betty were. Then, her gaze fixed on one table with alarm.

Betty noticed. "Is something wrong?"

"I need to leave. I … I just saw somebody I don't want to talk to."

That somebody was a man who resembled her uncle Jack, her father's brother. While growing up, she hadn't seen Jack very often, but occasionally he'd shown up during hunting season. He brought his hounds in the back of a pickup, and he and her dad went racoon hunting. He was dark-skinned with black, slicked-back, shoulder-length hair. His usual expression bordered on menace. Frances had never seen him smile. Though he looked like a movie star villain—a little like Jack Palance but not as handsome—he was supposedly on the side of the law. Her father said that he was a bounty hunter— a good one—who looked for wanted men and turned them into law officials. Her father regarded Jack with something akin to awe.

If the man was Uncle Jack—and she was fairly sure it was—there was a good chance her father had sent him to look for her. She didn't think he'd seen her, but she knew at once that she'd have to leave Cincinnati.

Where would she go? She thought of Cleveland, which was about as far north as she could go and still stay in Ohio. Moving to another state seemed daunting, although it might be a future possibility. She'd gone to Cleveland once with Roy. They took a boat ride on Lake Erie to Kelleys Island where they'd spent an afternoon strolling around an arts and crafts festival. Roy bought her a necklace made of shells that she thought was gaudy and later gave away to Good Will. In the evening, they ate perch sandwiches with fries and coleslaw and drank icy glasses of beer. She remembered reading on a restaurant menu that the name for coleslaw came from the Dutch expression *koosla* which meant "cabbage salad." Roy had promised to take her even farther north sometime—to Canada and to see Niagara Falls from the Canadian side in Ontario. They never made it there.

At the boarding house, she notified her landlady that she was leaving and left a message for her supervisor at work. Then, she called for bus schedules and found she could catch a bus to Cleveland, early the next afternoon. That wasn't soon enough, but it would have to do. She slept fitfully and woke up tired but knew she could sleep on the bus. In Cleveland, she stayed in a motel for four days until she found a suitable place to live. She was glad that she had been tight with her money, for she had enough to put down a deposit on a small apartment. She was tired of living in a rooming house.

She found a job as a waitress in a café near the Cleveland Clinic while she looked for a better job. A month later, she had a job at the clinic, doing similar work to that which she'd done in Cincinnati. She had a fresh start and felt confident enough to let her hair grow back to its natural red—with a little help from Clairol. Eventually, she discovered the Merlin Studio, where she was welcomed into a circle of regulars.

CHAPTER 3

Small-town Girl

Elizabeth met Jim, her future husband, when she took a job in the marketing department of a daily city newspaper. She had just graduated from a community college where she completed a course of business study. He was doing a summer internship as a clerk, while working on his bachelor's degree in journalism.

Elizabeth's father was a foundry worker, her mother a clerical worker in an elementary school office. They lived in a small town in a ranch house with three small bedrooms, one of which she shared with a sister three years younger than she. Her brother got a bedroom of his own, and, of course, the third belonged to her parents. There was little money for extras, but Elizabeth never felt deprived.

She lived a normal, pleasant small-town life until the end of her sophomore year in high school when a tragedy befell the family. Her father was diagnosed with Parkinson's disease. He went on disability, and family income was greatly reduced. Her younger brother and sister helped with paper routes. Elizabeth worked as a cashier in a drugstore on weekends. Her dream was to attend the state university, but that was no longer possible. With a part-time job, a student loan, and her mother's encouragement, she managed to go to a 2-year community college.

When she graduated, she saw the posting for the newspaper position listed in the college career placement office. It was 70 miles from home in Cleveland, but she hadn't found any local jobs that were appealing. A city newspaper sounded exciting. She applied but felt guilty. She should be close to home to help her mother and her siblings. When she got the job offer, she had second thoughts and almost turned it down. Then, she decided to bring it up with her mother, who was supportive as usual.

She told Elizabeth that she thought her father would have to go to a nursing home soon and that she should go about living her life. Elizabeth found an apartment that she shared with another young woman and started her life in the city with eagerness, though there were times she had painful moments of tears and sadness over her father. She tried to go home on weekends as often as she could afford bus fare.

Then, she met Jim, who had a very warm way of relating to people and making them laugh—a characteristic that was to make him an excellent reporter. Because he was friendly with everyone and maybe because she was so preoccupied with learning her job and still worried about her family, Elizabeth, at first, didn't consider his conversations with her as special attention. But one day, a co-worker said, "You know, he's got a crush on you." Elizabeth blushed and stammered. "Oh, I'm not sure of that."

When he got around to asking her out, he was straightforward. "I'm an intern and don't have much money, but could we, well, get together and do something, like take a walk in the park and sit on a bench and talk and maybe feed the ducks some breadcrumbs?"

She laughed and accepted.

When she told Jim about her father, he was visibly moved. His eyes brimmed with tears. He drove an old car that he said was held together with "duct tape and baling wire" and offered to drive her home on a weekend. "I'm pretty sure it'll hold together for that distance. If you've got a couch for me to sleep on … or I can bring along my old sleeping bag."

She called her mother to ask if it was okay, and she, of course, wanted to know if this was a serious relationship.

"I don't know, Mom. I think, well, maybe…."

Her family liked him, as she knew they would, and he was tender with her father and helped her take him outside and walk, though his mobility was now severely limited. Her father's face was expressionless, a condition she'd learned was called "facial masking" when the facial muscles became immobilized.

Jim asked her if she and her mother had objections to his writing an article about Parkinson's, using her family as a portrait of its effects on its victims and their families. He would submit it to the editor in charge of the health section. They agreed to let him do it, and the article was accepted and praised by the editor and others at the newspaper.

He might have been offered a job anyway after his internship, but the article cemented it—and their relationship. They were married in a no-frills ceremony in the Methodist Church Elizabeth's family attended.

She had worked the first two years of their marriage to help support them while he completed his master's degree. Then, she became a fulltime housewife and mother. Her daughter Leah was born, and two years later, Jim Jr., who was now a newspaper reporter himself in Florida.

She felt fortunate in her marriage. As the years passed and other couples they knew broke up and remarried other people, they joked that people found them boring because they were still in their first marriage.

Jim was always entertaining. He had many funny anecdotes about the peccadilloes of local politicians or the exploits of a brash, young reporter. She never tired of listening to his colorful stories, many of which he repeated numerous times.

But there had been a time when she wondered if he might be bored with her.

When the children were in their teens, she started taking courses at the local university. Although she'd always wanted to do that, she'd never admitted to anyone that the final impetus was motivated by jealousy. She thought Jim had mentioned a young female reporter admiringly too many times. She wanted to keep his interest, to be intellectually stimulating.

Her main frustration for the last several years of her marriage was his smoking habit. Cigarettes, along with endless cups of black coffee, were companions and stress reducers during the long stretches of waiting for news, interviewing, researching, writing, editing, rewriting, interjected by adrenaline rushes to cover a crime, an accident, or a conflagration, and, of course, the daily publishing deadline.

Even after a mild heart attack and a warning from his physician, Jim had refused to quit smoking. Six months after the first attack, he was found slumped over his desk by a coworker and had died before the emergency squad reached him. In her grieving, she'd dealt with a lot of anger about his smoking. Why hadn't he cared enough about his family to protect his health?

Elizabeth cocooned herself in her house, going out only for necessary things like groceries—and sometimes even asking Leah to get food items for her so she wouldn't have to go out.

Leah grew increasingly concerned about her mother. She thought she'd grown agoraphobic. She contacted her brother Jim who came to visit, and they did an intervention of sorts. They persuaded Elizabeth to get involved with fund-raising for Parkinson's, the disease that had taken their grandfather. It was a tactic designed to get Elizabeth out of the house and interested in a greater cause.

At first, Elizabeth was reluctant, but then she made friends with another volunteer, a cheerful, outgoing person and a dancer, who invited Elizabeth to attend a Saturday evening dance party at the Merlin Studio.

CHAPTER 4

Doctor and Nurse

Edith locked eyes with the intern standing in the middle of the group. Flustered, she blushed and averted her gaze to the patient, an 11-year-old boy who was making good progress in his struggle against leukemia and who looked uncomfortable being the center of attention. The lead doctor placed his hand reassuringly on the boy's shoulder and tried to put him at ease by asking about the St. Louis Cardinals, his favorite baseball team.

Edith was in her second year as an RN and was assigned to work in the children's unit of the hospital. Accompanying a more experienced nurse on her rounds with a doctor and the interns, she was to observe and learn.

Before rounds were over, Edith managed to see the intern's name tag—B. Sawyer—and his left hand which wore no wedding ring.

Later, she checked hospital staff information and found out the 'B' stood for Ben. Ben—she liked the name. It connoted strength and stability. Those were the qualities she thought she saw in her brief encounter. A man of medium height, nice looking, not quite handsome, but with direct blue eyes that conveyed self-assurance. He appeared in her daydreams, and she wondered when, not if, she would meet him again. Instinct told her he would be in her future.

Usually, Edith was not one to be preoccupied with her appearance. She concentrated on being competent and getting things done. Now, she took to standing in front of the mirror and examining herself critically. She knew she was not considered pretty, but her mother had always told her she was handsome. She had good bone structure and natural, dark blonde hair. Would Ben Sawyer find her appealing?

Four weeks later, just when she was beginning to think her instinct was wrong, Ben showed up at the hospital. He was to do a year's internship there.

She was assigned to one of his patients, a 9-year-old girl who suffered a concussion and a broken leg in an automobile accident in which her 5-year-old brother had been killed. Her mother, the driver, had sustained minor injuries. The girl was depressed and desperately needed the support of her family, but the parents were in a state of shock and grief over the son and didn't seem to be able to offer her the psychological support she needed. Edith saw that Ben, like herself, tried to give the girl extra attention. One day, the girl's grandmother, who lived in a different state, sailed in and took charge. Edith and Ben smiled at each other in relief as they watched the girl's mood improve under the grandmother's loving attention.

Shortly afterward, Ben asked Edith to have coffee with him in the hospital cafeteria.

He told her that he wanted to complete the present one-year internship, and then become a resident for another year in a different setting. Ultimately, he wanted to be a general practitioner but wanted to become as proficient as possible before taking that step. Although he liked working with children, he wanted to treat a variety of patients. Edith herself had begun to feel that maybe she wasn't cut out to work exclusively with sick children. Sometimes, she found it too heart-wrenching. They found commonality in talking about future career possibilities.

Soon, they were having coffee breaks together 2-3 times a week. Then, he asked her out on a real date, which got postponed because he was called in on an emergency. But finally, it happened.

Six months later, they were serious, and sometimes, Ben spent the night in her apartment. They talked about marriage, but Ben wanted to wait until after he finished his residency. He said he'd seen too many instances in which a wife supported her husband during internship and residency, and then, when the doctor began his career, the marriage ended, leaving people to think that the wife had been exploited. He didn't want people to think that Edith was supporting him financially.

Edith boldly proposed that Ben move in with her. Even if it was the Sixties when relationship norms were being broken, it felt quite daring. After a few weeks of thinking about it, he agreed. For professional reasons—they thought it better that their co-workers not know—they were quiet about it.

Things proceeded according to plan. Ben finished his residency and shared a practice with another doctor. They married and within a year, Edith was pregnant with Nancy. Two years later, Ben, Jr. came along.

Nancy was a bright little girl, and it was a delight to watch her grow and progress. But at age three, they began to realize that something was not right with Benjie, as they called him.

He spoke only a couple of words, didn't relate to his sister's overtures to play, and was fascinated with twirling ropes and strings. He was diagnosed with autism. As educated as they were about medical matters, Ben and Edith felt helpless. They began the endless rounds of counseling, speech therapy, and psychological testing. Professional people were all too ready to intellectualize the problem but offered little practical advice.

Ben was busy and involved in the process of setting up an independent practice, so Benjie's care and training fell mostly to Edith. She often felt drained, isolated, and mildly depressed. By the time Benjie was five, he was able to go to a special needs, pre-school program part-time. Edith had a few precious hours for herself. At first, she reveled in the quiet and freedom. She read novels, shopped for some new clothes, and took long walks. Soon, though, she found herself wishing for professional stimulation. She told Ben that she wanted to help in his practice. She assisted with billing service and filled in as a nurse when needed.

As Benjie grew, he learned to read and write, though not at his age level. He talked, but his vocabulary was limited, and he sometimes repeated words or phrases incessantly—a condition called echolalia. His social skills were severely limited, and Edith began to realize that she was his anchor. She was his intermediary to the world. Ben, though a dutiful father, was awkward with his son. His delight in Nancy's achievements contrasted with his relationship with Benjie. Edith had idealized her husband, thought he was nearly perfect, and she had to come to terms with her disappointment that Ben just wasn't going to be as interested and involved in Benjie's development as much as she would have liked. At times, she felt resentful, but she also took pride in helping Benjie reach his small achievements.

Throughout the years, they had made a good pair professionally. Edith played a crucial part in making Ben's practice run efficiently and effectively. Nancy was an honor student and well-rounded in her interests, running on the track team and excelling in academics. In her junior year in college, she became interested in psychology and told her parents that she wanted to major in the field. Ben was disappointed. He'd thought that she would follow in his footsteps and become a physician. Edith was secretly pleased. She thought that having a brother like Benjie had influenced Nancy to become interested in mental and developmental matters. She'd been involved in her own world, and Edith felt she was sometimes ashamed of Benjie when she was younger. But Nancy began to take more of an interest in him and was influential in finding training for him to hold down a part-time, janitorial job at a MacDonald's restaurant, where his need to have things in order was an asset.

At age 55, Ben had a successful practice, Benjie was doing okay, and their lives were going well. Ben had what he referred to as a "nervous gut"—not exactly a genuine medical diagnosis—which was acting up again. So, he did what he usually did—avoided spicy, hot foods and alcohol. Years ago, he'd had an attack of acute pancreatitis. He'd been told to avoid alcohol or to use it in moderation. He'd never abused alcohol but really enjoyed a glass or two of wine in the evening and an occasional martini, and that certainly qualified as moderation. He lost some weight which he attributed to his new eating habits. Then, his back began to bother him, too, and, at Edith's urging, for the doctor did not like to be a patient, went for an examination. He expected the doctor to recommend the food and drink habits he was already following and maybe more exercise and less work—in short, a mild regimen. But a blood test revealed higher levels of a certain antigen, and the doctor wanted him to have imaging tests. A CT and an MRI revealed abnormalities, and a biopsy confirmed pancreatic cancer—one of the deadliest malignancies. Their contented life became a nightmare. First, surgery, followed by chemotherapy and radiation, and, finally, palliative care. Ben died 18 months after his diagnosis.

As a nurse, Edith was on familiar terms with death. She had witnessed it and the grief it left in its wake many times. She'd seen it in the young, the middle-aged, and the elderly. Its visitation often seemed unjust, unfair, and cruel in its indifference. And medical people had to develop defense mechanisms. Sometimes, it meant becoming a little numb, and even, for some, especially emergency room personnel, using morbid humor—making jokes that would seem callous to outsiders. It was always a struggle to respond to death and bereavement with compassion and support, while maintaining one's own equilibrium. She and Ben had always tried hard to do that.

After Ben's death, some of that training, that mind set, helped. She tried to be strong for Benjie and Nancy and to take care of all the legal matters surrounding the medical practice with methodical efficiency. But six months or so after his death, she found it difficult to function in the practical way that was her nature. She became forgetful and was surprised when she was charged late fees for some ordinary, recurring bills. She neglected her personal hygiene, sometimes not taking a shower for three days. She'd never been one to spend time watching daytime television, but now she left the TV on a good part of the day. It didn't matter whether it was game shows or soap operas, she needed the TV on mostly for background noise. Her attention to what was happening in the programs was erratic, even for *General Hospital*. The only thing that concentrated her attention was Benjie's care. She saw that he was fed and clothed and managed to play checkers with him some evenings, always letting him win.

When Nancy came home one day and found her mother vague and unfocused with straggly, unwashed hair, she insisted that she see a grief counselor. One of the things the counselor recommended was getting out of the house more, even if it was just taking a walk. The counselor said, "Turn off the TV. Go outside. Get some exercise. Take a walk, look around you and observe what's going on. Go to Starbucks and have a latte, or whatever, with a friend if possible. Just simple things can be a start toward healing."

So, Edith started to walk. She even bought an expensive pair of walking shoes. In an adjacent neighborhood that she didn't often visit, she discovered a Fred Astaire dance studio with a picture window where she could watch students learning to dance and, on Friday evenings, see a dance party that was just for fun. She found herself going there more and more often. Watching the dancers, she longed for some type of meaningful connection.

Finally, it occurred to her one day that maybe she could take dance lessons. She'd never thought much about dancing before, but it would be exercise and please her counselor.

Feigning more courage than she possessed, she went into the studio one day and asked about lessons. They would be expensive, but what the heck? She signed up for private lessons with an instructor named Steve.

CHAPTER 5

Independent Traveler Abroad

Waiting in line to present her boarding pass, Joan suddenly felt light-headed.

Her first thought: *Oh God, I might be having a stroke.* Then quickly, *Get a grip! Control your anxiety.*

The anxiety was not from being afraid she might die with a group of strangers—all of them becoming tidbits for sharks when the plane plunged into the Atlantic Ocean. Well, maybe partly that, but she figured it was mostly other things.

She'd felt so brave and independent, a widow signing up for a three-week, London/Paris tour by herself, but it was her first transatlantic trip without Evan's comforting presence. Although they sometimes bickered, they'd generally been good traveling companions. Other than Montreal, Canada, they'd taken only one foreign trip. That had been to England ten years ago.

What if she missed some vital information and didn't connect with the tour? What if she somehow hadn't dotted all the i's and crossed the t's? What if she became stranded somewhere? What if she suddenly became ill? She and Evan had had each other to rely on and usually were able to figure things out.

And there was that other thing that gnawed at her. While Evan was still living, how many times had she thought about just leaving—disappearing, going she wasn't sure where? Some mornings she'd wake up with an overwhelming desire to flee, start a new life without Evan, without the messiness of their kids' lives.

She could almost feel the anticipation, the jolt in her chest when the plane started to rise. Then, she'd remember she was 53 years old. Women her age didn't disappear into new lives, did they? And, yes, she'd felt guilty about having those feelings. She couldn't quite let go of the residual guilt and enjoy the trip she was on now.

Her flight fantasies had remained fantasies. She sublimated her urges and listened to Joni Mitchell: *I get the urge for going but I never seem to go.*

She stayed because he was a good man, a generous man in some ways. Several years ago, she had quit her job as an administrative assistant to a state representative—a job that paid good money—and followed her yearning to be an artist. He'd hardly blinked when she told him what she was considering. He supported her, saying they would get by. And they did—get by. More than just get by. She had gained a local reputation as an artist and was able to show her work at several exhibits, making modest sales. She stayed because the two of them represented stability to two grandchildren whose parents couldn't provide it for them. Because he loved and had seemingly endless patience with his schizophrenic daughter even as she rejected him and accused him of "giving information to my enemies." And because his body was still warm and comforting next to her at night. And because she was afraid of the unknown. And then he had died suddenly of a heart attack and her guilt was compounded. For several months, she'd been bereft, immobilized.

On the plane, she gave up the self-analysis. *Let it be, Let it be.* She slept lightly, dozing and waking several times for the first two hours, and then after the less than appetizing dinner was served, fell blessedly into a deep sleep. Usually, that wasn't the case on airplanes.

At Heathrow, she was proud to know the drill. She was able to put aside her nervousness and go confidently through the passport validation line. Maybe that's why she'd chosen to start her trip in London, which was familiar, even though it had been a long time since she'd been here. She was relieved to spot the tour people holding up their signs. They told her where to meet the van driver who would take her to London after she got her luggage.

Thus far, things were working seamlessly.

Seven people were scrunched together in the van—a young couple, and two older couples near Joan's age. No one wanted to talk except one older, pleasantly plump woman, who introduced herself to the young woman. "Hello, I'm Emma from Iowa. Is this your first trip abroad?" The young woman said that she had spent a summer in France a few years ago and revealed that she and her husband were on their honeymoon, which delighted Emma. "Oh my, what a wonderful way to start a marriage! Our congratulations! Isn't that wonderful, Fred?" she said, addressing her husband. Joan and the other couple joined in and offered their congratulations as well. Emma then told everyone that it was the first time they'd been out of the states—well together at least. Her husband had been stationed in Germany many years ago when he was in the army. They were celebrating their 40th anniversary. And, of course, everyone offered congratulations to them on their anniversary. The man smiled and patted his wife on the back. Joan got the feeling he tolerated his wife's chatter but would rather sit alone in silence.

Emma turned her attention to Joan. "You're traveling by yourself? My, how brave you are." There was more pity than admiration in her voice.

"Oh, not brave, really. I've been here before." She didn't offer any further details.

"Are you staying with friends or relatives?"

"Emma, look, I think I can see the city ahead," her husband interrupted, craning his head toward the windshield.

Emma focused on the window momentarily to please Fred but soon turned to the other couple.

"And where are you people from?"

Thank you, Fred, for rescuing me. Joan didn't feel like indulging Emma's need to socialize and hoped that Bob and Mary from Omaha would keep her occupied until they got to the hotel. She wanted to escape to her room, look over the tour information, maybe watch a program on BBC, and take a nap before dinner time.

###

For dinner, she walked to a nearby pub and decided to try shepherd's pie, a dish made from ground lamb and vegetables with a crust of mashed potatoes. The menu described its history as a variation of "cottage pie," which appeared in 1791 when potatoes became an affordable staple for poor people. "Cottage" was a term for a modest dwelling in a rural setting. Later, the term "shepherd" was used when lamb was used instead of beef because shepherds tended sheep, not cows. The history was interesting, but the dish was too heavy and bland. She regretted not ordering fish and chips. She remembered eating fish and chips from a food vendor with Evan outside the Tower of London. It had tasted especially good, and they sometimes ordered it at a local pub near their home, although it was never quite as good as when they'd eaten it that day in London.

She recalled the other places they'd seen on that trip. Westminster Abbey only from the outside because a special event was being held there that day, and come to think of it, Parliament and Buckingham Palace, where they'd seen the changing of the Palace Guard, from the outside, too. And, of course, they'd toured the bloody Tower of London, site of unimaginable past horrors. They'd taken a day trip to Winchester and seen the famous cathedral, and then traveled on to the mysterious Stonehenge, less imposing in its reality than she had imagined.

This time, she would stay with the tour for scheduled sightseeing, certainly Stratford-on-Avon and Oxford and the town of Windsor with the Royal Castle but strike out on her own on two free days. She had decided to be a tourist of art and literature. She wanted to visit Poet's Corner in Westminster Abbey and possibly see a play at Shakespeare's Globe Theater. She wanted to be awed by the paintings hanging in the National Gallery. And she wanted to find some vantage points—she imagined sitting on a bench in a park with pigeons strutting around her—to make her own sketches of London life and landmarks. Would she have time to do all that? For a moment, she wished that she'd had the courage to make the trip by herself instead of on a tour ... but, no, she needed the structure, felt safer this way. And then, of course, the tour would move on to Paris—an intrigue she had not experienced before. She would not want to navigate Paris by herself.

At the end of six days, she had accomplished most of her solo endeavors. She'd toured the Globe Theater but was disappointed that no play was being performed that day. After leaving the Globe, she wandered along the walkway by the Thames and found some nice vantage points for sketching the city. There, she could see sleek, modern buildings, and, in contrast, the top of the medieval Tower of London, and the venerable London Bridge. Another day, she'd reveled in the art in the National Gallery for more than four hours.

Signing up for this tour, she'd thought more about being safe than socializing, but she had begun having pangs of loneliness, so she made efforts to be friendly with people in the tour group. Two women who were traveling together adopted her. They ate together at a café in Windsor and wandered around Oxford together, where scenes from Inspector Morse occupied Joan's imagination—though she'd read that not all the series had been filmed at Oxford. Then, on to Stratford-on-Avon where they toured the homes linked to Shakespeare and his family, including Anne Hathaway's picturesque, thatched-roof farmhouse, nestled among lovely gardens.

The tour arranged for coach transportation to Dover, where they took a ferry to Calais, and gave a great view of the rugged coastline with the famed White Cliffs of Dover. In Calais, a town nearly razed by the Germans in World War II, they boarded another coach for a 2-hour drive to the "City of Light."

The hotel was located only a couple of blocks from the Eiffel Tower. Joan, with Ellen and Sandy, her two new friends, ate lunch at the café on top of the Tower and made plans to go to go on an excursion to see Monet's home at Giverny.

When they boarded the bus for Giverny, Ellen and Sandy slipped in a seat about halfway back and Joan sat across from them in a seat by herself. As she slid into her seat, she noticed Emma and Fred, the couple from the airport van were in the seat back of her. She nodded and said hello. Fred nodded and Emma smiled broadly.

In a few minutes, Emma reached around the seat and patted Joan's shoulder. She said, "It's nice to see you found some friends." She nodded at Ellen and Sandy.

"Oh, yes, thank you. And I hope you have enjoyed the tour."

"Oh my, have we ever. Versailles was really something, wasn't it? All that wealth. My, my, and the common people lived in such poverty. That's why there was a revolution, our guide said."

"Yes, that's true." Joan wanted to be nice, but this woman got on her nerves. She had her pegged as a well-meaning busybody. "Well, I hope you will like visiting Monet's home."

"Our guide recommended it. I don't know much about art, but it will be interesting."

"I'm sure you will enjoy the beauty of the gardens. Be sure to have someone photograph you on one of the garden bridges," said Sandy, turning to join the conversation.

Emma smiled and turned to her husband, "Did you hear that, Fred? We'll have to ask someone to take our picture."

###

The day before the tour ended, Joan got up early and went to the hotel breakfast, which, as usual, had a wonderful selection of food. She chose *pain beurrée et confiture d'abricot*—a sliced baguette with butter and apricot jam—*café au lait*, and *jus d'orange pressé*—fresh orange juice. She had delighted in learning some common French words and phrases—especially food and drink. She had her tray and was just about to be seated when Emma waved from a table.

"Come join us. We'd love to have you."

This was not what Joan wanted to do. She wanted to sit alone with her breakfast and look at a travel book. Today, she planned to go to the Champs-Élysées, the grand boulevard with the Arc de Triomphe, and she wanted to navigate the Metro all by herself. The guidebook would give her some pointers.

But—*oh, what the hell, Joan. Just go sit with them a few minutes and then you can escape.* So, reluctantly, she took her tray to their table. They told her that their children—two sons and a daughter—had given them this trip for their 40th anniversary. And she told them that her husband had died two years ago of a heart attack. She told herself that snubbing them would have ruined her day, and it wasn't really that bad. So, as soon as she had finished most of her breakfast—she would have liked a refill of the *café au lait*—she excused herself and went outside and found a bench where she could browse her guidebook before boarding the Metro.

That evening, Joan grabbed a crepe and soda from a small café. At the hotel, a singer and pianist duo were performing in the lounge. She ordered a glass of Merlot and sat by herself basking in the atmosphere. The singer alternated singing in

French and English. Joan thumbed through her guidebook. She had fallen in love with Paris and wasn't ready to leave.

"Hello—"

She looked up, surprised to see Fred standing by her table with a cocktail in his hand.

"Mind if I sit down?" And he sat—without waiting for her answer.

"Where is Emma?"

"She's asleep. She has arthritis, you know. Too much walking gets to her."

"Well. I was just—"

He interjected, "Look, er, I thought you might ... maybe we could go to your room for a while. you know, order a bottle of vino, and keep each other company.

He leaned toward her in a conspiratorial way with an alcoholic gleam.

"I don't think that's a good idea," she said, jumping up. She grabbed her purse and guidebook, almost spilling her half-downed drink.

"Wait, I mean ... I just thought you might be lonely," he called after her as she strode toward the elevator.

The next morning, she went down to meet the van that was to take part of the tour group to the airport. She hoped Emma and Fred would not be in the van. But there they were. As the bus driver was helping Emma board the bus, Fred sidled over to Joan.

"Sorry, sorry ... I had too much to drink. Please don't say anything to Emma," he pleaded.

She wanted to say, "You weren't that drunk. You're just a jerk! And you ruined my last evening in Paris." But for Emma's sake—she could see her smiling and waving from a bus window—she did not want to make a scene or appear angry, so she just stepped over to the van and asked the driver if she could sit in the front passenger seat where she wouldn't have to look at or be in contact with the couple.

On the flight home, she congratulated herself on a successful solo trip—well, successful except for the incident last evening that still left her feeling icky. She'd been told by friends to watch out for the French Lotharios. Instead, she'd had to fend off advances from a drunk American.

Briefly, she entertained the possibility that something about her had given Fred the idea he could make advances. Some signal that she wasn't aware of maybe. In the cramped airplane toilet, she examined herself in the small mirror. Before the trip, she'd contemplated letting her hair go gray but decided to dye it light brown again. The graying process, she knew, would be somewhat difficult, and she didn't need that extra stress on the trip. She'd gotten a cut that was pixie-ish and easy care, one that she could make a bit spiky with some gel. It suited her slender build, and she thought she'd keep it that way when she did get up the nerve to go gray. She could see nothing in the mirror that suggested allurement. If anything, she thought—hoped—she appeared "artistic," which she was.

But enough! She would put all these thoughts aside. She would not blame herself for the actions of a sleaze bag, who assumed that a "deprived" widow would welcome his advances. She'd not been looking for a sordid tryst.

An image of Evan working in the yard came to her. She was flooded with a sense of tenderness. She wondered if he'd ever suspected her flight fantasies. If he did, he kept his suspicions to himself, for that was his way. He would probably have thought her fantasies were just that—passing thoughts borne out of frustration. She'd felt guilt and regret. And now he was gone, and yes, she missed his companionship, missed the many ways he had been important to her and the family.

She wished she'd signed up for a lengthier tour. She would like to see Roman fountains, Swiss chalets, and what was left of the Berlin Wall.

Though she'd rather not be going home, she knew it would be a lot easier than it once would have been. Her son Ray and his wife Marta were now divorced. Marta had cheated on him numerous times in none-too-discreet ways. Yet, when they separated, Ray fell apart. He drank and smoked too much and often came home late in the evenings, leaving Evan and her in charge of the 8-year-old twins, Nora and Nick. When he was around, the twins often fended for themselves, and Ray took little interest in their schoolwork, expecting Evan and Joan to take care of that, too. But after Evan died, Ray surprised her. He sobered up and became responsible. Recently, he became engaged to a woman who cared for him and the kids, who were now teenagers and had weathered all the dysfunction surprisingly well.

Her daughter Ellen was in a stable period, too. Ellen had been diagnosed with schizophrenia at the age of 21, in her junior year in college. There'd been periods when she refused to take medication because she said it made her gain weight. The paranoia started in college. She wanted to be an artist like her mother, but it wasn't working out. Her projects got mediocre grades, and her relationship with her instructors deteriorated. She got in a rather public argument with some other art students. She'd had to drop out of school. Then, her paranoia started to include her family. Voices sometimes told her that she couldn't trust them—that she needed to get away. She fled to the street where there were truly few people to be trusted. Much of her paranoia was directed at Evan. She said he didn't want her to be an artist and had somehow conspired with her college instructors. But when she was well, she favored him over Joan. When he died, she went into a downward spiral and ran away. One night Joan received a call from the police in Toronto, Canada. They had found Ellen on the street. She'd been beaten and robbed of the few possessions she had. Ray, now channeling his father, had gone to Toronto and brought her home. They never knew how she had managed to get to Canada. Now, Ellen was back on her meds and had a job that involved entering data into computers. And, miracle of miracles, she had a boyfriend, a skinny, nerdish guy with a thin face and nice hair with a wave like Elvis Presley, with whom he was obsessed. He seemed devoted to Ellen, didn't mind her extra pounds, and wanted to take her to visit Graceland.

With the much-welcomed family stability, Joan had felt free to sign up for the tour. And soon, too soon, she would be home, although she'd caught the "travel bug" and hoped she would be traveling again soon.

Unable to sleep, she looked through the film offerings on the plane and decided on a Japanese film, entitled *Let's Dance.* She found it so charming and funny that it made her want to explore the world of ballroom dancing. Maybe she would look up 'ballroom dancing' in the yellow pages when she got home.

CHAPTER 6

Novice Dancer

Approaching the intersection at Main and Second Avenue, Elizabeth eyed the elegant, dancing couple framed in neon that no longer lit. She'd always thought the sign faded, aged like the interior of the Merlin Dance Studio itself. But now, poised above a slightly sagging, black canopy in the mid-afternoon drizzle, the dancers seemed vivid and animated. Eyeing them between swipes of the windshield wipers, Elizabeth imagined the man in black tux and the woman in flowing red gown moving to their own rhythm.

The dashing couple vanished from sight, replaced by a mental image of Art and herself, dancing the rumba to Julio Iglesias' "Hey." Skillfully, Art leads her into an underarm turn; then, holding hands, free arms extended outward, they glide forward, synchronized in a slow, quick, quick Cuban rhythm.

The performance at Merlin Studio was captured on video during a practice session about six months ago. Elizabeth has not been to the studio for four months. She and Art are no longer partners. Though they were dance partners only, not romantic partners, the circumstances of becoming "unpartnered" were unpleasant.

Feeling something akin to self-pity welling up, she abruptly switched off the video image. She hadn't expected this charge of emotion. It had tripped her up like a new dance step when the brain understands what to do but the feet haven't yet got the message.

She parked the car and turned off the engine but felt immobilized—unable to make the effort to go out into the rain and climb the stairs to the studio to a Sunday afternoon social dance.

She pictured the studio—the ceiling glitter ball, the Chinese lanterns, and the miniature silvery white lights on branches stuck in large vases, the mirror-lined walls, and the photographs of smiling dancers.

Elizabeth had started going to the Merlin studio for lessons about two years ago. At age 54, she'd been a widow for two years. A friend had talked her into trying ballroom dancing as a social activity.

She was surprised to find that she had a talent for dancing. Except for dancing at high school proms, she'd rarely been on a dance floor. Maybe she'd absorbed some moves from Fred and Ginger, Gene Kelly and Cyd Charisse, Doris Day and Gene Nelson—the dancers in all those old musicals she'd loved.

After the first several lessons, she'd been paired with Art, an experienced amateur. It was the studio's practice to ask the more accomplished students to help teach the novices. Dancing became even more satisfying because she had a regular partner whose movements she learned to anticipate and complement. Art led her firmly, with sureness and economy of movement.

Elizabeth knew little about her dance partner, other than someone said he was divorced. Art was polite, but quiet, self-contained, almost aloof. He seldom laughed but had a nice smile that radiated from his eyes, subtly softening his otherwise sober demeanor. Of medium height, with graying hair and a moustache that seemed an integral part of his face, he was approximately her age, but had the slender build of a younger man. They never saw each other outside the dance hall except when he walked her to her car after their lesson or a couple of times when several people from the class went dancing at a local nightclub after class.

They danced so well that they were asked to be the entertainment at show time for one of the studio's weekly Saturday night dance parties. That time, they bounced, strutted, turned, and twisted through a triple swing. Vera Moore, the owner of the studio, said they did so well that they should prepare another exhibition, the rumba perhaps, and they began to practice each Wednesday night for an hour after the regular group lesson was over.

On a snowy Saturday evening about a month before the scheduled exhibition, a woman Elizabeth had never seen before came to the dance. When she entered, she attracted little attention. If anything, the people who looked her way might have thought her somewhat down-at-the-heels. She had on a long coat that looked rather worn, a pair of practical, lined, low-heeled boots, and a woven, plaid scarf that loosely covered her hair and tied under her chin.

She disappeared directly into the ladies' lounge and reappeared a few minutes later in a stunning transformation. She looked about 5'10" in 3-inch heels, had long shapely legs, slender hips, and a Marilyn Monroe bosom. All her assets were displayed to advantage by a bright blue, fitted dress with a side slit above the knee. Her hair was of medium length, permed, auburn-dyed, framing a pretty, though not beautiful heart-shaped face and large brown eyes. She appeared to be in her late thirties, with only the slight lines around the mouth hinting that she might be older.

She stood at the end of the dance floor, packaged to be noticed, yet somehow detached. She surveyed the dancers and swept her gaze briefly across the group of single women, including Elizabeth, who were sitting together on one side of the room. She appeared not to even consider the possibility of joining them.

At any rate, she didn't need to think much about sitting, for, within a few minutes, the men discovered her. Attracted by her looks, they also found that she was a good dancer, who had a beguiling smile and a way of concentrating on each of them in turn, making them feel special.

It was as though a spotlight followed her as she glided around the dance floor with successive partners. The single women, always a majority over the number of male partners, noted her with envy as they pretended not to watch. The gossip grapevine quickly went into action. Georgia was her name, and she had come to the studio a few years ago for lessons. She was separated from her husband, a man reputed to be a wonderful dancer, but an alcoholic who abused her.

Elizabeth watched Art watching Georgia as she danced with other men. After she had danced several times with others, he made his way toward her. She turned to him with her radiant smile, and he smiled back in his way of not quite smiling but with lights flickering in his eyes. Their eyes locked as they began to dance.

Painfully fascinated, Elizabeth watched them, and thought about the scene in *Picnic* in which Kim Novak and William Holden dance together in sensual discovery.

The rumba ended, and they stayed together for a fox trot.

Frances, an attractive redhead who seemed to delight in couples' intrigue, nudged Elizabeth. "Look at your partner!"

Elizabeth was relieved when another man claimed Georgia for the next dance, a waltz, and Art came to ask her to dance. They danced well, but dispassionately. Elizabeth felt inhibited, and he seemed distracted, hardly meeting her eyes.

After the waltz, Elizabeth escaped to the women's lounge. She sat down in front of the mirror, put her elbows on the counter, cupped her face in her hands, and closed her eyes.

She felt embarrassed and angry at herself for reacting this way. She still mourned her husband, Jim, and hadn't been consciously aware of any romantic feelings toward Art. Now though, seeing him with Georgia, she knew that she'd grown dependent on his company, at least, in the confines of the dance studio. He was a special dance partner, and she liked to think that she was special to him, too.

Someone pushed the door to enter the lounge, and Elizabeth quickly looked into the mirror, smoothing her hair. She stood up and looked at herself critically. Her petite, slender, small-bosomed figure always had been a source of pride, but now she thought she just looked shrunken. Her fine gray hair worn in a natural, blow-dry style seemed merely matronly, not attractive as her husband Jim had always said it was. She felt both old and adolescent.

Taking a deep breath, she steeled herself to return to the dance. Under Frances's scrutiny, she wanted to appear nonchalant. She danced in the 10 o'clock circle, smiling gaily at her partners and, shortly afterward, made her excuses to leave.

Frances leaned toward her conspiratorially. "I'll watch Art for you!" she said, rolling her eyes.

It took only two weeks before Art told Vera that his schedule had changed, and he could no longer come to the Wednesday evening class Elizabeth attended, and, sorry, but he wouldn't be able to practice for a rumba exhibition either. To Elizabeth he said nothing. Seemingly, he was insensitive to any feelings she might have about suddenly being dropped as a dance partner.

Vera, who had encouraged many would-be dancers with two left feet and soothed hurt feelings of others in similar situations, asked Elizabeth if she would be a helper and dance with a new male student who had signed up for a beginning class and had no partner.

Three weeks later, Frances reported that Art and Georgia had signed up together for an advanced class on another night.

Elizabeth started dancing with the beginner, Ed, a shy man in his late thirties, who, though not naturally rhythmic, seemed determined to become a good dancer. She liked Ed, but just wasn't up to teaching him. She had to force cheerfulness and encouragement.

Two weeks later, when she came down with the flu, Elizabeth almost welcomed the illness as a respite. She needed to withdraw, grieve anew for Jim, sort out her feelings, and reexamine her life.

On the sixth day, she began to recover. Her daughter, Leah, a nurse who worked at a nearby hospital, swept cheerily into the house, bringing some videos.

"You're looking much better today, Mom. I thought you might feel like watching a movie."

She held up two Fred Astaire/Ginger Rogers videos.

"You need to get well so you can do another exhibition with— What's his name? Remember, I get to come and see the next one."

Uh-oh. She'd never told Leah about Art's defection, and she didn't feel like telling her now.

"Well, we'll see," she dissembled. "I don't think I'm going to feel like dancing for a while."

In the following weeks, she used weakness as an excuse not to return to the dance studio, but she was starting to feel like a whiner, and Leah was urging her to go for a medical checkup. She was afraid that she was reverting to agoraphobia.

That's when Elizabeth decided to screw up her courage and attend this Sunday afternoon dance. But now she sat watching the rivulets of rain on her windshield, feeling melancholic and considering leaving without going inside.

She saw a familiar figure crossing the street—a flash of red hair under a purple umbrella. Frances spied her and started waving vigorously. She tapped on the car window and commanded, "Come on in!" Elizabeth rolled down the window slightly and laughed despite herself. "Okay, okay, just give me a minute here."

When Elizabeth walked into the studio, she wondered why she'd been so hesitant. People welcomed her, and she was in demand on the dance floor. Soon, it was as though she'd never been absent. Frances, who Elizabeth had once regarded warily, was genuinely friendly and warm. Elizabeth decided that her tendency to be smart-alecky and snide was a defense mechanism.

Elizabeth found herself dancing with a new man who introduced himself as Carl Gilman. The first two times she had paid little attention to him. He was pleasant, probably a few years older than she, of medium height, and though not obese, carried an extra 10-15 pounds. His most striking feature was a healthy head of silvery gray hair. On the dance floor, he was limited to the two-step and the waltz, performing both in a methodical way. By the third dance, he began to talk more.

"Do you come here often?" he asked, using the standard intro line that the women sometimes joked about among themselves.

He told her that he hadn't danced for many years and that he'd lost his wife to cancer two years ago. Later, she found him beside her as she got some coffee and a snack from the *hors d'œuvre* table.

Having found the return to the studio painless, even pleasant, she returned the next Saturday and again found Carl Gilman present and attentive. He brought her coffee and told her that he was retired from fulltime work, but now did software consulting for businesses. She wasn't surprised when he asked if she would have dinner with him before the dance the following Saturday.

Later, Frances commented, "Well, I see you have a new friend. I danced with him in the circle, and he's no Fred Astaire!"

On Tuesday, Vera, the studio proprietor, called and asked if she would consider coming back to Wednesday group classes and dancing with Ed. Elizabeth said yes.

On their first date, Carl took her to Humboldt's, a highly rated restaurant located on the top floor of a high-rise building. They had a window table with a great view of the city and an extraordinary meal of roast duck in orange sauce. They talked about their former spouses. He and his wife and been happily married for twenty-five years, he said, and she told him about Jim, who was a newspaper reporter, a heavy smoker who had died suddenly of a heart attack. Once or twice, they were both on the verge of tears.

During the next month, he continued to ask her out. He treated her with an old-fashioned gallantry that amused her. Once, they went dancing on Saturday night, but it didn't work out well. As his date, she didn't feel free to dance with others, and she began to realize that he didn't enjoy dancing much.

Meanwhile, Ed asked her to dance the rumba with him in the "Spring Fling," the studio's annual showcase. She said she'd think about it.

On Sunday, when she saw Carl, she told him about the invitation, explaining to him how the studio paired new dancers with more experienced dancers. She even mentioned Art and their swing exhibition.

"You must be a pretty good dancer?"

"I do okay," she laughed.

He wanted to know about Art and Ed, how old they were. He approved of Art, but of Ed, he said, "Well, maybe Vera could find someone his age."

She wasn't sure what reaction she expected, but she felt chastened.

A week later, she told him that she'd decided she wasn't ready to have a steady relationship with a man. Could they be friends? See each other occasionally? She wasn't sure this was possible, but she wanted to be amicable, to let him save face. He looked disappointed but seemed to take it well.

At the dance party, the following Saturday, Elizabeth looked over a partner's shoulder and did a double take. Art came in without Georgia on his arm.

As soon as possible, Frances rushed to tell her that Georgia had left Art and returned to her husband. She was excited, and Elizabeth wondered if Frances really thought she'd be interested in pursuing Art as a partner again.

After Art had danced with others a few times, he crossed the room and extended his arm to her. "Dance?"

She rose hesitantly, and he locked her firmly in his smooth, confident lead.

After a few moments, he seemed to remember that it would be polite to make small talk. "Still taking lessons?" he asked.

"Yes. Yes," she said making up her mind on the moment, "I'm going to be dancing in the spring showcase."

His eyes flickered on hers for a moment, something surfacing momentarily before disappearing back into dark waters.

"Oh," he said, "That's good." He didn't ask what dance or who her dance partner would be.

Carl Gilman came and danced with other women, but barely acknowledged her.

Sitting out a dance, she watched the couples circle the floor, enjoying a sense of familiarity with their individual styles. An attorney who spent a handsome amount on private lessons with his striking, blond-plaited partner; they were easily the most professional dancers on the floor. An older man whose bent posture broke all the rules of good dance form but danced with such authority that he was considered a good dancer. A young couple who were fairly new dancers, so awkward and bouncy they made her wince, but they seemed to be proud of their beginning accomplishments.

As the dancers moved buoyantly around the floor to the beat of Jimmy Buffett's "Margaritaville," Elizabeth sat in their midst, momentarily alone, but with a sense of equanimity, feeling like she had passed an initiation rite and now belonged here.

A line of poetry once studied in a literature class floated through her mind. "How can we tell the dancer from the dance?" William Butler Yeats. She couldn't remember the prof's interpretation, something high-minded about a theory of art.

Then, Ed, who had become more outgoing as his dance skills had improved, was extending his hand.

"You look like you're thinking way too much," he teased.

"I think you're so right!" she said, smiling confidently, as he guided her firmly to the floor.

CHAPTER 7

Private Dancer

Edith's private lessons with Steve began with the fox trot and the single swing. She felt awkward at first, but Steve's voice was like soft butter, gently encouraging her. His corrections didn't seem like corrections. She began to look forward to the lessons. They moved onto the waltz, her favorite. She knew the basic box step because she and Ben had learned it long ago for their wedding dance, so they moved onto some more advanced steps. She lost her self-consciousness and relaxed into following his firm, confident lead.

One day, as they were finishing up their lesson, a guy came in and stood watching them. Steve smiled at him and said, "Tom, look how great Edith is doing. She just started a month ago."

Edith blushed and fumbled a step. "Sorry," she said.

Tom said, "You're doing great. Steve is a wonderful teacher." He seemed to sense that his watching was making her nervous, and he disappeared into a back room.

When the lesson was over, Edith went to the bathroom and then stayed to chat with a female instructor with whom she'd gotten friendly.

Steve raised his hand to say goodbye. "Good lesson, Edith. We'll start on the rumba, next Wednesday. See you then." He left with Tom.

"Is that Steve's brother?" Edith asked.

The instructor smiled. "That's his partner, dear … his lover."

"Oh … Oh dear, I…"

"Does that shock you? I didn't mean to. There are many wonderful male dancers who are gay."

"No, I … just wasn't thinking. Of course … it's fine."

She didn't want to be narrow-minded, but something changed. It wasn't that she had entertained romantic feelings about Steve, who was probably 10-15 years younger than she, but she did have romantic feelings—heterosexual in nature—about ballroom dancing, and she was disillusioned.

When she finished the set of five lessons for which she'd signed up, she told Steve that she was busy with other things and needed to take a break from dancing.

CHAPTER 8

Friends with Commonalities

Joan and Edith met at a local outdoor arts festival where Joan was exhibiting her work.

Edith had Benjie with her, and he saw a painting Joan had done of two horses by a barn. The horses had their heads together as if being playful with each other. Benjie was developing a fascination for horses. Her daughter Nancy had told Edith that sometimes people with autism responded to being around them, grooming and riding them. She had found a horse farm that had activities for people with disabilities and had taken him there a few times.

Edith bought the painting to hang in Benjie's room, and she and Joan began to talk. They had in common that they were both widows who had a child with problems. They became friends.

Joan had read an article about ballroom dancing in the local paper's special senior's section. It had profiled Vera Moore and the Merlin Studio. When she found out that Edith had taken some private dance lessons—and sensed that she missed them—she told her about the article and wondered if they might go there together on a Saturday evening to see what it was like. Joan herself had never danced, but she remembered the film *Shall We Dance?* that she had seen on the plane returning from her London/Paris tour and thought so charming. The Studio had a group lesson before the dance party, and, with Edith's help, she thought maybe she could learn a few steps.

So, Edith and Joan went to the dance party, and there they met Frances and Elizabeth. The seeds for the Merlin Subsidiary were sewn.

CHAPTER 9

Tango Enthusiast

In a yellow taxicab with her husband Bao on their way to a midtown Manhattan hotel, Cecilia Wang already felt the excitement of the city—the throngs of people at intersections, street vendors and performers, ethnic restaurants, and chic boutiques with artistic window displays. There was a light rain, but the day was not dreary. Streetlights and headlights reflected off the multitude of yellow taxis, making the scene quite cheerful, in Cecilia's opinion. The rain and a bobbing sea of umbrellas only added to the mystique she felt for the city. She was energized—a sensation she did not often experience in the Midwest. The "Big Apple." The "city that never sleeps." It was going to be a good vacation.

Bao, a professor of information science at a university, was presenting a paper at a conference. For a few hours each day, she would be free to shop and explore the city by herself, or perhaps in the company of the wife of one of Bao's colleagues who was also attending the conference.

Bao had been reared by strict, penurious parents in the outskirts of Shanghai. They had tried to arrange a marriage for him with the daughter of a family they had known for some years, but then, Bao had gotten the chance to attend graduate school in the United States and told his parents he wanted to postpone marriage.

In the States, he met Cecilia, an American-born Chinese, at a mixer. When he received his Ph.D., the university sponsored him for a green card, and he asked her to marry him.

The Wangs had been married for fifteen years and had no children. Though he never said so, Cecilia wondered if he was disappointed at not having an heir, but that thought had not led her to stop using birth control. Cecilia herself was not unhappy being childless. She was an RN and regarded her patients as her children, but she could leave the responsibility for them to other medical personnel when she left work. She enjoyed her free time.

Exploring the city, Cecilia came upon a marquee advertising *Forever Tango*. A poster in the window showed dancers in a seductive pose. The female dancer had ruby lips, high cheek bones, black hair pulled back in a chignon, and wore a sexy, silver lamé dress. The male had jet black hair with a wave on the side and wore a sleek black shirt and hip-hugging pants. Her back was to him, hips to crotch, and her arms stretched back to his face in a caressing motion. His hand with splayed fingers grasped her midriff possessively. Cecilia was aroused, not just by the sexiness of the couple, but by something akin to aesthetic appreciation. She knew she had to see *Forever Tango*.

Back at the hotel, she found a brochure that described the show: "*Forever Tango* features the history of the tango through music, dance, song and dramatic vignettes. The dance couples are accompanied by an on-stage orchestra that includes musicians who play the bandoneon, a small accordion-like instrument with a melancholy sound unique to the tango."

She persuaded Bao and another couple to attend the show. Bao, who had never danced or, for that matter, given dancing, much less the tango, any thought, found the show too provocative for his tastes. Seated beside him, Cecilia seemed unaware of him. It was as though she was surrounded by an invisible force field. As he watched her profile, he knew that she was transfixed, enraptured by what she was seeing on stage, and it gave him a sense of regret. He sensed a vivacity that had drawn him to her when they'd first met but that had been muted by the ordinariness of their lives. He wished that they'd had a child who might have brought renewed vitality and closeness.

If Bao experienced a sense of foreboding that he couldn't name, he was correct. His wife was to become obsessed with the Argentine tango, and it would play a major role in their eventual separation and divorce.

CHAPTER 10

A Disturbing Tale

Cecilia had a mysterious air and didn't divulge much about her personal life.

While the members of the group had fun gossiping and poking fun of the foibles of some of the dance studio regulars, Cecilia usually sat quietly smiling.

"Do you think we're awful, Cecilia? The way we talk and laugh at people? You're always so quiet." said Elizabeth one evening.

"Oh, no, I enjoy it. I just like to sit here and be *inscrutable*," she said—smiling as usual.

The other women glanced at each other. Then, they noted the gleam in Cecilia's eye and burst out laughing. Cecilia beamed in appreciation that they got her "stereotype" joke.

"I was wondering, Cecilia … about your name. Were you named after St. Cecilia?" asked Joan.

"Have you heard of the famous Mandarin restaurant in San Francisco?"

"I think I saw a program about it once ... on CBS *Sunday Morning*, maybe. They interviewed the owner, a woman."

"Yes, there was a TV program. The Mandarin was owned by Cecilia Chiang—my namesake. She is a grand lady and a smart businesswoman. It is a great honor to be named after her. She was given a Chinese name when she was born, but when she went to a Catholic University, she took the name Cecilia. She was a relative of my mother. They both grew up in China. I don't know if you know much about Chinese history. I don't want to bore you—"

"Oh no, we're not bored. This is so interesting. Please tell us more," said Elizabeth.

The others murmured in agreement.

"As young girls, they grew up in privileged families when General Chiang Kai-shek was in power. But then the Japanese invaded during World War II and privileged families lost so much. After the Japanese came the Communists. Their families were reduced to poverty. Cecilia and one of her sisters walked for weeks and weeks to get to free China... Then, they went to Shanghai.

"Cecilia and her husband and daughter were on the last plane out of Shanghai just before the Communists took over in 1949, I believe. It was a narrow escape. Her husband Chiang Liang was a businessman who had connections in government. He was planning for them to go to Taiwan, but then he was offered a diplomatic position in Tokyo. Cecilia Chiang did not want to go because she still saw the Japanese as enemies, but Chiang Liang convinced her that most Japanese were nice people.

"In Tokyo, she and her friends and acquaintances missed the food from her homeland, and she started a successful restaurant called The Forbidden City and lived a comfortable life in Tokyo for about ten years. In 1960, she came to San Francisco to visit a sister. The Mandarin was started by accident. Cecilia Chiang befriended some women who wanted to start a restaurant by giving them a loan of $10,000 to secure their rent. The women backed out, and the landlord refused to refund the money, so Cecilia Chiang started The Mandarin. It, too, became a great success."

"Did your mother come to the States, too?"

"Yes, she escaped to Taiwan where she met and married my father, who was an ABC." Cecilia Wang paused and smiled.

"On ABC?" queried Joan.

"No, *an ABC*. It stands for American Born Chinese.

"My mother and Cecilia were fortunate… My mother's sister… This is hard to talk about— She was forced to be a 'comfort woman' for Japanese soldiers. She later committed suicide."

"A 'comfort woman'?" asked Frances.

Cecilia Wang looked discomfited.

Edith, who had felt a special kinship with Cecilia since she found out she was a nurse, reached over and took her hand. To the others, she explained, "It means that she was forced to provide sex to Japanese soldiers. I read about it somewhere."

They all began consoling Cecilia by saying how awful that was. Then, they fell into stunned silence. Cecilia Wang had given them a disturbing glimpse into the horrors that can befall women in war time.

"Next time we meet, I will prepare a recipe for us from Cecilia Chiang's book." Cecilia broke the silence, and the group was grateful to turn from a subject they didn't like to think about.

CHAPTER 11

A Change in Attitude

Edith didn't feel like doing the Electric Slide. She was tired of it. Vera should give it a rest for a while. Still, she had to admit, it always drew several people to the floor.

It was a good time for a bathroom break. She entered the small bathroom that had two narrow stalls and, annoyingly, no hooks on which to hang purses. She would suggest that improvement to Vera, though she doubted she would spend the money to have it done.

One stall was occupied, and when she entered the empty stall, she became aware of a sniffling sound coming from the other side. She thought the woman there was trying to stifle her sobs.

Thinking it was none of her business, Edith washed her hands and left the bathroom but then changed her mind and went back in.

"Are you okay?" she asked, tapping on the door of the stall. "Could I help you in some way?"

"No." The woman's voice wavered. "I'm okay ... just a bit upset, that's all."

"Sure?"

"Yes." Then the woman asked, "Are you one of the group of single women that always sit together?"

"Yes, my name is Edith."

"You're not married?"

"No, I'm a widow."

"Oh, I'm sorry."

"That's okay."

"I guess I should consider myself lucky. I have a husband, and I love him. I'm just being foolish."

She came out of the stall, and Edith recognized her as one of the regulars at the studio. She and her husband almost always danced together, rarely changing partners or participating in the rounds. She was a better dancer than her husband, although he did okay. On a rare time when they had danced in a round, Edith had danced with him. She had the feeling that he was shy and didn't feel comfortable trying to lead women other than his wife.

"I'm Lucy, by the way." She paused. "I guess you might think I'm silly. I just get frustrated at times because my husband doesn't want to learn and improve his dancing. I take it more seriously than he does, and sometimes I feel I just want to stop dancing unless we get better at it."

"I don't think you're silly. Do you and your husband come for the half-hour lessons Vera offers before the dance starts?"

"Sometimes ... but he gets confused and cross when he doesn't understand the steps."

"Maybe private lessons, if you can afford them."

"I've thought of that. Maybe ... I'm embarrassed. I shouldn't be unloading on you."

"It's no problem. I hope you find a solution because I think you really do enjoy dancing."

She smiled. "Yes, I do. Well, I'd better fix my face and get back to the dance. Thanks for listening."

Edith left the restroom, and shortly after, Lucy came out and smiled at her husband who, Edith guessed, was a bit anxious that she had been gone so long.

Edith thought about sharing the incident with her friends, but she decided not to. It would be like betraying a confidence, she thought, even though she didn't know Lucy that well. As a nurse and a doctor's wife, she had been schooled to protect people's privacy, and sometimes that meant psychological, as well as medical information. Her natural inclination was to be discreet.

Edith felt some empathy toward Lucy. She understood her need for a certain level of mastery. She had felt, well, something akin to transported when she danced with Steve. She wondered amusedly what her husband Ben would have been like trying to do ballroom dancing. The only time they'd danced was to slow music at dinner parties with his physician colleagues. It was easy enough to imagine that he, a serious doctor, would not take dancing seriously.

Since she'd stopped taking private lessons with Steve, she had been given to self-examination. She had been taken aback to learn that he was gay, and she was distressed to think that her reaction might mean an anti-gay bias. In the medical field, she had encountered a broad range of people, conditions, and issues. She thought of herself as just, fair, and broad-minded.

There was no denying that the revelation had upended some of her ideas about ballroom dancing—ideas that had been subconscious for the most part. A part of it, she supposed, was romanticism. It was not that she had romantic ideas about Steve himself, for he was several years younger than she. It was the kind of romanticism that was imbued in the culture. Fred Astaire and Ginger Rogers' films were its best representatives. Was she still stuck in the thirties and forties in some ways? No, she didn't think so. It was more like she just hadn't been paying attention to what was going on in dance and pop culture.

Now she strived for a more objective, updated view. She started watching *Dancing with the Stars* and televised programs of professional ballroom dancing competitions, and she realized that what the female instructor at the dance studio had told her was true. There were a great many gay ballroom dancers with female partners. She watched the film *Shall We Dance?* that had a gay dancer in it. Her new view became more about the pleasure of dance itself—the rhythm, the learning of steps and executing them, and the sheer exhilaration of movement with a partner in a coordinated way. In a way, she decided, it was like learning a sport.

CHAPTER 12

Mistress of the Tango

Cecilia Wang was a thin wisp of a woman who wore miniskirts the others would dare not wear to dances. Sometimes she wore them with black tights, sometimes just ecru hosiery. Somehow, she carried it off because she was so slender and generally looked solemn—not like she was trying to be sexy. She had chiseled features and short, dark hair with a wave swathed across her forehead. On the dance floor, Cecilia was so wispy and light that she seemed to float in the arms of her partners.

She loved ballroom dance in general but was passionate about the Argentine tango. She took private lessons and sometimes did exhibitions with a man who specialized in the dance. He was at least ten years her junior. Their performances were dramatic with kicks, whirls, dips, and spins. Sometimes they organized *milongas*—tango parties. She explained other tango terms and demonstrated some dance moves to the Merlin Subsidiary group. Ganchos were leg hooks; giros were turns; and ochos were figure eights.

Doing the Argentine, Cecilia became exotic—at times almost demonic. At her first exhibition, Joan, the observer, who tried to be broad-minded and tolerant, was still shocked the first time she saw Cecilia with her right leg hooked over her partner's left knee and her left leg stretched back against the guy's other extended leg while he arched her backwards with a piercing gaze. Edith gasped. Elizabeth crossed her legs and lowered her eyes. Frances smiled. She liked discovering the uninhibited side of Cecilia's personality.

Later, Frances whispered, "My god, she gave her twat a stretch!"

The grapevine suspicions of Cecilia's marital status were now confirmed. She and her husband Bao got divorced. Sometimes she came to the dance on Saturdays with the "tango man," as her friends called him, but sometimes, too, with another younger partner—who was also good at the Argentine tango. The Merlin Subsidiary thought that she was probably not romantically involved with either of the men. She just liked to dance.

"It happens. She loved dancing more than she loved her boob of a husband," quipped Frances.

CHAPTER 13

Dinner, Talk, & DWTS

Edith wanted to prepare a formal, candlelight dinner for her Merlin friends. She had once been proficient at holding such dinners and had received many compliments from Ben and their circle of friends and acquaintances. It would be a "plated" dinner. This meant that the entrée would be served with the food already on the plate when it was brought to the table, as opposed to buffet style or family style in which dishes are passed around the table for people to help themselves. Plating, she told them also referred to the placement of food on the plate to make it attractive. It was very important in food photography. For instance, the placement of entrée food should be arranged by thinking of a clock face: The starch should be at 10 o'clock, the protein at 3 o'clock, and the vegetables between 3 and 9 o'clock.

At first, there was the feeling that she might be showing off, showing her social superiority, whether she was conscious of it as such.

Frances said maybe she was "putting on airs."

But then they found out that Edith had taken a course from a well-known chef who had taught her a lot about food presentation and being a good hostess. She had learned to be a decent cook from her mother, but she had learned several niceties from the chef.

Elizabeth said, "I think she just wants to do something nice for us—and maybe show off her skills as well. If I'd learned some things from a chef, I'd want to show off, too."

The dinner was planned for a Monday evening before the finale of the current season of *Dancing of the Stars*, which they enjoyed watching together. The first course was an arugula salad with a vinaigrette dressing, followed by an entrée of seared pork tenderloin with chive mashed potatoes and baby carrots. Dessert was a chocolate soufflé with orange sauce, dressed up with a drizzle of raspberry sauce. Edith refused their offers of help and served everything herself—from the guest's left as was proper. Everything looked gorgeous and tasted wonderful.

After dinner, they relaxed and finished off a bottle of *Pinot Noir*.

Now more at ease, Edith became talkative. She told them that the last time she was at the Merlin, she'd danced with a guy who told her he was in the business of supplying Porta Potty units to concerts and festivals. "Imagine that! And I was married to a doctor." The others laughed at her indignation, and she didn't seem to mind. She'd meant to amuse them.

Then, there was some gentle teasing of Elizabeth about Ed, the guy she'd danced with when she first came to the studio. She had helped teach him to dance, and it was obvious, they noted, that she was still his favorite partner. "Oh, for heaven's sake, he's only a few years older than my son," she responded. She didn't tell them that he had recently asked her out for dinner and a movie.

After a lull in the conversation, Cecilia solemnly told them something personal.

"Bao has a new woman." She went on. "And my friend says they are expecting a baby. They will be married sometime soon."

They weren't sure how to respond. She sensed their unease.

"It is okay. I didn't want children … and I like to dance … and he didn't."

And she left it at that.

But they were left wondering if it was okay because after she made her announcement, she retreated into her "inscrutable" shell. She was quieter than usual as they watched DWTS—a raucous gathering in which they rooted for and criticized the dancers, made predictions, called in their votes, tried to pre-guess the judges, and sometimes got to their feet and screamed at Len Goodman, the judge who was the most miserly with his scores.

CHAPTER 14

Private Again

Joan dropped by Edith's house late on a Thursday morning. She'd been diagnosed with osteopenia, and she wanted to ask Edith's opinion on treatment.

Benjie answered the door.

"Hi Benjie. Is your mom here?"

"No."

"Do you work today?"

"Yes, 1 o'clock."

"So, your mom will be back soon to take you to work?"

"Yes. She told me not to let anyone in the house."

"Your mom's right. I'll come back later."

"She will come soon to take me to work… She went to the dance place with the big window."

"Oh … Okay, I will see her another time. Bye, Benjie."

The dance place with the big window? That wasn't the Merlin. Hmm, Joan wondered if he meant the Fred Astaire Studio where Edith had first taken private lessons. Curious, she drove by the studio and saw Edith's car parked nearby. She could see a couple dancing but wasn't close enough to see if the woman was Edith.

Edith didn't come to their last group meeting, and she hadn't been to the Merlin for the last two Saturdays. Joan had decided to drop by her house, not only to get medical advice, but also just to see if she was okay.

Now, she thought she knew why Edith hadn't come to the Merlin. Benjie had spilled the beans. She had returned to taking private lessons at the Fred Astaire Studio.

She told the other members of the Merlin Subsidiary her suspicion. They wondered if it meant that Edith would not come to the Merlin anymore—if she would drop out of their group. It was no secret that she sometimes didn't like the choice of partners she found at the Merlin.

Joan thought that Edith would tell them about returning to her private lessons when she felt ready to tell them, so they shouldn't let their suspicions be known. She also thought that Edith would still come to their group, even if she didn't come to the Merlin Studio.

CHAPTER 15

Blackpool

Joan had a plan, a presentation to make.

She'd been to England twice, and she wanted to go again, and she wanted to take some friends with her.

She had become more and more interested in all things English. She liked British comedies and mysteries and the BBC. She liked studying about English literature and the history of the English language. She liked Queen Elizabeth and Prince Phillip—though the rest of the family, not so much. Edith told her she was an Anglophile.

In the film *Shall We Dance?* she had learned about Blackpool, the seaside resort that could be reached by a 3-hour train ride from London. The famous Blackpool Tower housed an opulent ballroom, where an annual international ballroom dancing contest was held. Her mission was to persuade the members of the Merlin Subsidiary to take a trip to England and visit the ballroom—during the dance competition, if possible.

To convince them, she showed photos and videos from the Internet and laid out an itinerary. They could start in London and see all the usual landmarks, then go to Blackpool, and then maybe to Liverpool, home of the Beatles.

All agreed that such a trip sounded exciting. Elizabeth said without hesitation that she'd like to go, which surprised Joan, for she didn't usually think of her as adventurous. Cecilia and Fran still worked part-time but said they'd like to go if they could arrange a schedule with their employers. Edith was the only other one who'd been to England. She'd gone to London once with Ben to a medical conference. She said she'd consider it if she could make appropriate arrangements for Benjie.

Joan was sure the plan would come together after a few more discussions.

CHAPTER 16

The Sailor

There were three things most Merlin Ballroom frequenters knew about Dick Morris. He was a good dancer, he loved to dance, and his wife didn't. He came most Saturday nights, usually without her. No one believed that he had any ideas about dalliances with other women. It was just accepted that he came because he liked to dance. The single women appreciated him and his dancing skill.

One Saturday, he brought a guy with him and introduced him as Wade, his brother-in-law who was visiting, on shore leave from the Navy. Unlike Dick, who had a modest demeanor, Wade had a sailor's swagger and a gait that spoke of sea legs.

Shortly, it became apparent that he had that indefinable quality known as "presence" on the dance floor. It wasn't so much that he knew a great many steps, but what he did know, he executed with bravado.

It also became apparent that his favorite dance partner was the only redhead in the room. That was Frances. She wore a bright green dress and looked striking. When she and Wade danced a swing, they diminished the other dancers and captivated the room.

Wade came to the dance again the following Saturday. He was said to have extended his leave. Joan and Elizabeth noted a familiarity between Wade and Frances who looked at him with dewy eyes.

"Do you think she saw him this week?" asked Elizabeth.

"I would bet on it."

"Do you trust him?"

"No."

A month later, Wade turned up again. People wondered if maybe he was no longer in the Navy. Maybe he'd been discharged. Otherwise, how could he take so many leaves?

The week after that, Joan, Elizabeth, Cecilia, and Frances were at the dance. Edith was not. She'd been coming less lately. Dick showed up late. Wade was not with him. Dick took Frances aside. He took her hands in his and appeared to be in serious conversation. When he left her side to dance, Frances grabbed her coat and stalked out. She didn't stop to say goodbye to the members of the Merlin Subsidiary.

Elizabeth said, "I'm going to see if I can catch her and see what's wrong." She put her coat on and left.

Joan pulled Dick aside. "What's wrong with Frances, do you know? Is it something about Wade?"

"Oh … I feel awful. I shouldn't ever have brought him here. I had to tell her that he was arrested for being AWOL. And that's not all! He has a wife and three children, though he's practically deserted them."

Elizabeth returned to the studio. "I was too late. She'd already gone."

Joan reported what Dick had told her. They all felt awful for Frances.

CHAPTER 17

Frances in Crisis

The sirens were coming closer and closer but not yet near enough. Not fast enough!

Joan stood at the window, her heart pounding, her body taut, as Edith tended to Frances. They'd found an empty Xanax bottle on the kitchen counter and Frances crumpled on the floor unconscious. They'd assumed cause and effect.

The group had been surprised that Frances hadn't shown up at their monthly gathering because it was a special occasion—Edith's birthday. There'd been presents and a special cake. They'd tried to call but got no answer. Edith wanted to take Frances a piece of cake. They put the cake in a closed container and thought they'd leave it by her door if she wasn't home. She didn't answer the door, but Edith turned the knob and found the door unlocked. She'd called, "Frances, it's Edith and Joan. Are you here? Frances . . .?" Edith had a vague premonition that something wasn't right, and they entered the apartment.

They'd found Frances supine on the bedroom floor, her red hair partially matted in yellowish vomit. Edith immediately went into nurse emergency mode. She took Frances's pulse, listened to her chest, and checked her airway.

"Her pulse is a little slow, but she's breathing okay. Call 911! Tell them it's a possible drug overdose."

She grabbed a box of tissues from the table to wipe the vomit away from Frances's face and sent Joan scurrying for wet cloths.

"And look to see if there's any evidence that she might have been drinking alcohol. Alcohol and Xanax ingested together can be toxic."

Joan did as she was instructed and found a glass with partially melted ice cubes close to a bottle of vodka on the kitchen counter. "But the bottle is nearly full. That's good, huh?" Joan implored.

"Let's hope so. I need your help in turning her. I want to get her into what is called a recovery position."

She extended Frances's one arm at a right angle to her body with her palm up, and then she folded the other arm, so it was supporting her cheek. She put her left knee at a right angle and asked Joan to hold it in place while she rolled Frances to her side. She tilted her head back and lifted her chin.

"This will help prevent choking and keep her airway clear."

Edith talked to Frances in a soft but firm voice. "Frances, hon, it's Edith. Joan and I are here to help you. Can you cough?"

Frances gave a little cough and egested a small bit of vomit.

Frances's eyes opened briefly. Edith gave Joan a half smile that showed relief.

"I think she's coming around."

The reflection of strobe lights flashed crazily through the window. Joan watched as men piled out and ran for the entranceway to the apartment building. She ran out into the hallway to see if they needed direction. Then, suddenly they spilled into the room, two following behind the rest with a gurney.

Edith pointed to the empty bottle on the counter. "We think she overdosed on Xanax."

"Tried to off herself, huh? You all her relatives?"

"We're friends."

By occupation, these were men who witnessed a lot of human emergencies. They wore a mild callousness the way they wore their uniforms. Sure of themselves, showing little self-doubt, they concentrated on doing what was best for Frances until they could transport her to a hospital. Beyond basic courtesy, they didn't have the time or the vocabulary for tact and niceties of expression. They were guys you could imagine exchanging crude, humorous stories in taverns and pool halls.

Edith hovered as they started an IV. When the paramedic showed a bit of impatience with her, she identified herself as a nurse, and he quickly changed his attitude.

"She's in a good position—recovery position, they call it. Did you do that?"

"Yes."

They continued to talk about treatment. It became evident that Edith could converse in the lingo, the medical shorthand they used

If the situation hadn't been so dire, Joan might have found some irony in the fact that the Doctor's Wife, who showed mild disdain for some of the blue-collar guys she danced with at the Merlin Studio, communicated with these guys so easily.

The critical decision seemed to center on whether a certain drug should be injected intravenously. Joan had never heard of it. It sounded like flu . . . something. Edith was saying it could cause convulsions. She was concerned that they might administer it. The paramedic was on the phone with a doctor, presumably, and others were asking Edith questions about Frances' general health and her use of alcohol. Did she know if she had been combined Xanax with alcohol?

Edith came over to Joan and embraced her.

"I had no inkling that Frances was in such a sad state. Did you?"

"No, I didn't. Frances is usually good at putting on an act, making light of things."

Edith walked back to be near the paramedics but made sure she kept enough distance not to interfere with the treatment. Joan found out the correct spelling of flumazenil by searching for Xanax and overdose on her iPhone.

After the ambulance took Frances away, Joan asked about treatment.

"What about that drug—flu—something?

"Too much danger of a seizure. And she was regaining consciousness. They'll give her supportive care—start an IV, give her oxygen, possibly oral suctioning. The doctors at the hospital will decide if she needs other treatment." She paused. "They'll probably put her in the psychiatric unit to determine if she needs treatment."

"Oh God, Edith, what if we hadn't stopped in?"

"I know, I know."

Joan said to herself, thank God for Edith's premonitions. Thank God, Edith was a nurse.

Joan said she would stay with Benjie for a few days so Edith could spend more time with Frances. Frances, at first refused to admit that the overdose had been a suicide attempt.

She said it was a mistake, a miscalculation, but after a couple of days, she did admit to feeling "very down" before taking the Xanax.

Frances resisted the ministrations of her Merlin Subsidiary friends other than Edith, who reported that Joan was recovering nicely. The women thought they understood. Edith was a nurse who had helped save her life, and the more people she had to deal with, even those with whom she had a special connection, the more stressful it would be for her.

CHAPTER 18

Dancing at the Merlin

Joan was dancing with the Porta Potty guy, who was instructing her in a rumba step that he had all wrong. She was half listening and not in the mood to tactfully correct him. She looked over his shoulder and saw Frances come in the door. "Excuse me, I see a friend I need to say hello to." She left him standing in the middle of the floor.

She rushed to give Frances a bear hug, "Oh Fran, I'm so happy to see you." Cecilia and Elizabeth soon did the same thing. It was the first time Frances had come to the studio since she'd overdosed. She seemed happy and perfectly okay to bask in their attention.

Frances asked, "Edith isn't here?"

"No … actually, we haven't seen Edith for about a month. I called her, and she said she might come tonight," said Joan.

Just then, they turned and saw Edith come in, followed by two guys they'd not seen before.

"Speak of the devil!" said Joan.

Edith seemed to know the men, who had struck up a conversation with Vera, who also seemed to know them.

Then, they walked over to the group of women.

The two guys stood smiling behind Edith, while she hugged and greeted her friends. Then, Edith tugged one guy's arm. "This is Steve. He's my instructor at the Fred Astaire Studio, and this is his friend, Tom. They wanted to come with me to the Merlin to see what it's like. And, oh yes, guys, this is Joan, this is Frances, this is Cecilia, and this is Elizabeth. They'd all love to dance with you."

The guys were gracious and sure of themselves in the way dance instructors are, and soon they were taking turns escorting the women to the floor. When Steve and Edith did a foxtrot, the women oohed and aahed. Edith was flushed and confident, and they could understand—sort of—her return to private lessons.

Everyone had a good time, and it seemed a rather magical evening. Cecilia and her dance partner were a highlight when they performed a steamy Argentine tango for show time entertainment.

When Joan and Frances were sitting alone while the others danced, Frances looked at her and said, "I'm sorry for what I put you and Edith through…" She looked ready to burst into tears. Joan hugged her and shushed her. "It's okay, Fran. It's how it turned out that matters. Edith was heroic, but she would say she was just using her nursing skills."

Frances squeezed her hand and said, "I know. I know. She saved me. I'm in awe of her."

Then, she pulled Joan to the floor. "No more serious stuff. Come on, let's do the Electric Slide—Edith's favorite!" She rolled her eyes.

Later, Frances whispered in Joan's ear. "I'm all in for that Blackpool trip." ■

After Class

"**H**ey, Miz Patterson. Good class! See you next week!" Briana Jones yelled out the car window, her shrill voice competing with LL Cool J blaring from the radio. Then, the driver, probably the Ronald she wrote about in her personal essays—the one responsible for the bruises on her smooth, mocha arms—gunned the engine and sped away.

Grace Patterson smiled and waved as she walked to her car. She'd finished teaching her English Composition class at a small downtown business college. In a cynical mood, she thought Briana's compliment was a hopeful bribe that the carelessly written essay she turned in tonight would be graded leniently. *Sometimes I wonder why I'm not retired, or more accurately, why I didn't stay retired.*

Get a grip. It goes with the territory. She drew a deep breath. The classroom was stuffy tonight, and it felt good to be outside. In late September, even at 10 p.m., the air was still pleasantly mild.

She strode down the partially lit street, mindful of her posture. She knew the recommendations for discouraging a predator. Hold your head up, walk determinedly and quickly. She was not exactly uneasy, nor did she see anyone threatening; she was merely informed and cautious.

Grace had taken early retirement from her job at a state agency writing research proposals and had gone back to her first love, teaching. She usually got a great deal of satisfaction from working with the students who attended her classes. For many of them, the college represented a second chance. Some had been high school dropouts who later took the GED. Most had completed high school and had families to support. Many were single mothers, divorced or never married. They juggled work, childcare, and finances.

And what better thing should she be doing with her life? She and her husband of 25 years had long ago divorced. Her son, George Jr., lived in Cincinnati, and her daughter Karen, with whom she had a strained relationship, lived in Cleveland, both 3-4 hours away.

George, her former husband, had been an alcoholic, as her father had been. Her psychiatrist had tried to point this out subtly. "So Freudian!" he might as well have said.

Ironically, George's young second wife had apparently helped him find the strength to give up the bottle. Now, Karen reported that her dad attends AAA meetings and is a doting father to his 3-year-old daughter.

Grace and her son, George, Jr., who preferred to be called Ken, short for his middle name Kenneth, found these developments galling; they were unable to forgive and forget the years of shame from psychological and physical abuse. Karen, who had always seemed to be able to touch a soft part of her father not accessible to Ken and herself, was frequently in contact with him, establishing a relationship with the stepmother, who was not many years older than she, and her half-sister, who played with her own daughter, 4-year-old Connie.

Grace felt that Karen blamed her for not being able to provide whatever it was that her father needed to quit drinking.

Once, she had referred to her as "codependent." Stunned and hurt at Karen's attitude, Grace found it increasingly difficult to maintain a relationship with her. She was managing to do so, only because she wanted to see her granddaughter.

Her teaching made her feel useful and helped keep her mind off personal problems.

Bobby Ray Baker was cruising with his brother-in-law, Dale Jenkins. Both had had a few beers and a few tokes. Bobby Ray had been in several scrapes—brief jail stays for a DUI, drunken brawling in bars, and possession of a small amount of marijuana. Dale had served time for dealing drugs and had been out of prison for only two months. Aside from moderate drinking and smoking marijuana occasionally, he was trying to go straight for his family, wife Darla and two young sons. So far, he'd gotten only temporary day labor jobs, but he was hopeful something better would come along soon if he stayed out of trouble.

That night, Darla had kicked Bobby Ray out. She told him he was a bad influence, and she couldn't have him in her house anymore.

Dale said, "Okay, okay. I'll take him out and see if I can find him a place."

They parked in Dale's Ford truck in a dark corner of the First Methodist Church parking lot to finish a six pack. Bobby Ray was singing along with Garth Brooks's "I've Got Friends in Low Places," and reached over to turn up the volume.

"Hey, man, cool it!" Dale said. He turned the volume back down. "We don't want to attract no attention here."

"Oh hell, Dale, police ain't hanging around churches. They're out chasing the crim-i-nee-al element!"

"Just the same—ain't no use in takin' chances."

"You got any money for more rock, Dale?"

"Nah, just change. This six-pack did it."

Bobby Ray tapped his foot, keeping time with the music. "Look, I really need it, man."

"Can't be helped. Look, we got to get down to the homeless shelter before they close you out."

Bobby Ray rolled down the window and spat. "Here's what I think of the homeless shelter."

"Darla ain't gonna to let you in. She is definite. I know my wife."

"Darla don't love me no mo-o-re," Bobby Ray sings, then changes to "Roxanne, you don't have to put on the red light. You don't have to sell your body tonight."

"Shut up, Bobby Ray! Ain't gonna be no singing at the shelter." He starts the car.

"I see somebody! Maybe she can help me out." Bobby Ray opened the door and jumped out.

He has spotted Grace Patterson walking on the sidewalk between the church and the adjacent building.

"Damn it, Bobby Ray, don't! I don't want no trouble. You understand? Get back here!"

Bobby Ray darted into shadows where he could find them, watching her as she headed toward her car in the middle of the nearly empty lot.

Bobby Ray followed. A few feet from her car, she pushed the unlock button on her key, and he shouted, "How ya' doin' there, Miz Robinson?"

Shaken, she managed to respond in a rational tone. "You must have me confused with someone else. My name isn't Robinson."

"No, you're the one I want to see."

He was close enough that she could see the recklessness in his eyes and smell the alcohol on his breath. Trembling, she dashed for her car, but fumbled her keys dropping them on the pavement.

She reached down to grab them, but he snatched them first.

"Come on, Miz. Robinson, I'll trade you—keys for cash. Help out a poor addict." He dangled the keys in her face.

Grace still trembled, but not with fear. All her caution vanished, swept away by a furious brushfire of anger.

"I'm not giving my hard-earned money to a good-for-nothing drunk. I spent 25 years with a drunk like you. Leave me alone, you miserable sonofabitch! Get away from me! Get a job!"

"Don't you call me a sonofabitch!" Images of rejection from significant women swam through his drug-battered, alcohol-soaked brain. The ninth-grade English teacher he spat at before he walked out of school for good. His mother screaming at him that he was good-for-nothing like his father. His sister kicking him out of her house earlier in the evening.

He grabbed at her purse. She held on and kicked his shin. He plowed his fist into her jaw twice. She fell, hitting her head on the pavement. Then he kicked her once in the ribs.

Dale drove up, skidded to a stop, and jumped out of the car.

"Oh Jesus! Jesus, Bobby Ray, look what you've done done."

He jerked Bobby Ray away from Grace Patterson, then bent down to examine her. "Lady, lady," he pleads. "Say something."

No response. He began to cry. "Shit, Bobby Ray! Shit! What is the matter with you?"

"She shouldn't of talked back. She should've been smarter than that."

Dale felt for a pulse in her neck and got none.

"You in big shit now, Bobby Ray. *We* in big shit. She's *dead*."

"Nah, can't be. I just messed with her a little bit!"

"*She is dead!*"

"Nah, can't be." But now he's looking scared. "What we gonna do, Dale?"

"Let me think. Let me think."

Bobby Ray started to open Grace Patterson's car door.

Dale grabbed his arm. "Fingerprints, stupid! You ever watch CSI?"

Bobby Ray was now gulping deep breaths—hyperventilating. "Don't call me stupid!"

"Look, Bobby Ray, we got to get out of here. We got to get out of here quick!"

Glaring at Dale as though he was responsible for the whole mess, Bobby Ray held up the keys to the car and pushed the trunk button. He then bent down and put his hands under her armpits and dragged her to the trunk.

"Give me a hand, brother-in-law! You're in this, too." He clenched his fist menacingly.

Reluctantly, Dale reached into his truck, found an old pair of work gloves, and picked up her feet to help heave the body into the trunk. Bobby Ray wiped the keys with his shirttail and threw them in the trunk and closed it. Then, he picked up the purse from the pavement and jumped in Dale's truck. "Come on, Dale! Don't stand there like you're *stupid* or something!"

###

Grace Patterson's car went unnoticed for two days. Then, it was impounded. A wrecker hauled it away and her identity as owner was established by the license plate. A message was left on her phone, followed by a notice in the mail.

Ken Patterson also left a message on his mother's phone, Saturday, and wondered why she didn't return his call by Sunday evening. He called Karen who reluctantly agreed to make the trip to check on her mother if she could not be reached by Tuesday. On Monday night, Ken received a call from the dean of the business college. His mother hadn't shown up for work, hadn't called, and couldn't be reached by phone.

Ken called the police who searched the car and opened the trunk.

The police were unable to find witnesses or fingerprints. The case drew the attention of the local paper, which ran articles about Grace, quoting school administrators and some of her students: "Mrs. Patterson went out of her way to help me. Nobody taught me grammar in high school."

At the funeral, Ken sat alone, grim and ashen, a few seats away from his sister and her family. Earlier, he had planted himself in front of his father and threatened to make a scene if he and his new family came to the funeral. Karen protested, but, noting her brother's resolute fury, acquiesced, saying, "I'm sorry, Dad. Just go home, please!"

As the weeks wore on and the case went unsolved, the paper ran articles about the need for more police patrols in the downtown area. The school adopted a new policy that female workers who taught evening classes should have escorts to their cars.

###

Two years later …

Ken Patterson sat at his desk measuring the man across from him. As a public defender for the first seven years of his career, he had learned to keep his expression neutral and wait for the telling detail that would reveal the person. Now, Ken worked for a private law firm that specialized in environmental cases—a career that was much more satisfying to him in many ways—but sometimes he missed the adrenalin rush of his former job.

The man who introduced himself as Dale Jones had insisted on seeing Ken, saying that he had some important information about a case. Ken was skeptical but alert. He knew that valuable information sometimes came from unlikely sources. He suspected, though, that the man wanted to see him about something having to do with an old case he had handled while a public defender, a case no longer relevant to his interests.

Appraising Dale Jones' appearance, he saw a man who was about 5'7" and slight of build with light brown hair pulled back into a rubber-band secured ponytail. He wore baggy jeans and a jacket that looked too thin to keep him dry on a rainy spring day. He looked down and out but determined to do better. Evasive, but at the same time, earnest.

He began telling his story so obliquely that it took Ken a minute or two before he realized the man might be talking about his mother's murder. At that point, he abruptly leaned forward, fighting the urge to lunge across the desk, grab the man by the throat, and demand that he cut the roundabout crap and tell him everything he knew *NOW*.

Dale Jones wasn't stupid. He saw the anger, the tensing of Ken's body. Gripping the arms of the chair and readying himself for a quick exit, he said, "Look, man, I think maybe I made a mistake. Sorry for taking your time."

"No! No! Sit down! Look—if you know anything about Grace Patterson's death, tell me! If you didn't do it, I promise to do you no harm."

Dale Jones began again, and Ken knew that if he wanted to find out what Jones knew, he'd have to appear dispassionate and ask the right questions.

"It was my brother-in-law what did it."

"You mean," he swallowed, "killed Grace Patterson." He couldn't say *my mother*.

Jones nodded.

"How do you know he did it?"

"He tol' me. One night, him and me had a few beers, and he tol' me. Said he didna' mean to do it, the only time he ever killed anyone. A mistake. Swore me to secrecy"

"How do you know he was telling the truth? Maybe he just read about it in the paper and made up a story."

"He showed me the *proof*." He said *proof* in a self-important way that made Ken narrow his eyes.

"What proof?"

"Her purse and her driver's license."

Ken tensed but remained a sculpture of controlled emotion. The police had never released the information to the public that those items were missing.

"You're sure it was Grace Patterson's driver's license?"

"It had her name and her pitcher. The pitcher looked like the woman in the paper."

"This was over a year ago. And you still remember it? That's hard to believe."

"I … I just remember it, that's all. She was a teacher, warn't she?"

Ken sat unmoving and silent. Dale wanted to run again, but he was trapped by Ken's measuring glare.

"What is your brother-in-law's name?"

"Bobby Ray."

Finally, Ken, asked in the deliberately calm tone of an attorney, "Where is Bobby Ray? What is he doing now?"

As the conversation proceeded, Ken began to figure out why Dale Jones had come to him. This man, allegedly his mother's murderer, was blackmailing Jones to gain favors.

Jones' mother-in-law had died, leaving her 30-acre farm to Jones' wife, Darla. To Bobby Ray, her son, she had willed a sum of money that he quickly spent on liquor, drugs, and women.

They had the farm, but he didn't have a job. Darla had a job as a nurse's aide, but her salary didn't cover all the expenses. He said he wanted to go straight and not deal drugs, but because he needed money, he had planted marijuana on the back acres of the farm. Bobby Ray had found out and demanded a cut, or else he would tell Darla about Grace Patterson's murder. Now, he was camping in an old building on the property, but he wanted Jones to lean on Darla to let him live in the basement of the farmhouse. He wanted money, and he frequently wanted to borrow Jones's pickup which he drove while drinking.

"I come to you because I can't afford more trouble with the law. I … I just thought … you being a lawyer and all.

Maybe you'd know how to keep me out of it." He paused. "I unnerstand there's a reward."

Ken's ferocity returned. "Look, I need to see that purse and driver's license—*evidence,* you understand ..."

Stammering, Dale said, "Look, I ... I gotta check on it. I'll call you."

"When? When will you call?" He pulled a business card from a drawer and slid it across the desk. "How can I get in touch with you?"

"You can't call me. I'll call you back, I promise ... soon, maybe a week." Dale made a quick exit.

As soon as the door closed, Ken threw off his suit jacket, grabbed a lightweight hooded nylon jacket he sometimes used for jogging in cool weather, and ran to the stairwell. He ran down the ten levels, tying the hood tightly on his head and pulling it down as much as he could over his face. He also removed his reading glasses, shoving them into the jacket pocket.

He emerged from the stairwell just in time to see Dale's back disappearing out the revolving door. He followed Dale, stopping once to peer intently into the window of Macy's when Dale looked back over his shoulder. He was grateful that the day was overcast with a steady drizzle. Dale disappeared into a parking garage. Ken quickly ran to the garage exit and stationed himself nearby so he could have a clear view of the vehicles that came out of the garage. The third vehicle was Dale's pickup truck. Ken memorized the license number.

Back in his office, Ken reflected on how his mother's death had affected the family. His significant other, Charlotte, an attorney, had walked out on him. She told him he was withdrawn and morose and refused to get grief counseling.

Maybe that was true, but he'd expected her to care enough to stick with him. His sister Karen had also separated from her husband. She'd become somewhat paranoid in her thinking and believed her husband was unfaithful. He didn't know if this was true or not. Tall and striking, Karen had once worked part-time as a model for local retailers. Though she had nurses' training, she now worked only on temporary assignments—saying it was hard to deal with people's problems since her mother's death. Ken thought that Karen regretted her differences with their mother. Connie, his niece, was fearful and cried a lot. She didn't understand what happened to her grandma.

He fixed himself a fresh cup of coffee, his third of the day, and realized that something had come alive in him again.

The results of the license number search revealed that the truck belonged to a Dale Jenkins, not Dale Jones, and the address was in a rural area some 5-6 hours away. Now, Ken knew approximately where to locate Jenkins. For the first time, he had some real hope of solving his mother's murder.

Three days went by, and Ken hardly slept. He was in a state of manic alertness and self-doubt. He considered contacting the police but didn't. This was personal, and he wanted to see it through as far as he could before turning it over to the authorities. He'd seen how they'd bungled some cases.

On the following Saturday and subsequent weekends, Ken drove to the area. Partially disguising himself, he let his beard grow and wore a baseball cap, shabby clothing, and sunglasses. Through some discreet sleuthing, he determined that Bobby Ray was Bobby Ray Baker. He wondered if Dale

Jenkins (AKA, Dale Jones) had intentionally meant to give him the impression that Ray was the last name.

It was farm country with animal smells. There were many old farmhouses with peeling paint and grey weathered barns. Less often, there were well kept white houses and red barns with white trim. Some homes were trailers on concrete blocks with junk cars in the yard. The roads were straight and flat with farm fields on both sides but sometimes turned abruptly into sharp curves and hills in wooded areas. At one point, a road cut across a former quarry with steep sides and no fence or other barriers to prevent a car from plunging into the abyss.

Jenkins had told him that Bobby Ray borrowed his truck to go to a tavern on Saturday nights, so late on a Saturday afternoon, Ken parked his rental car on a dirt side road and watched the main road for Jenkins' truck. At 7 o'clock, the truck sped by, the baritone of George Jones floating from its open windows.

The truck was parked outside Joe's Bar & Grill. Ken walked in and slid into a booth where he could see the man he thought was Billy Ray sitting at the bar. The man was slender and of medium height. He had shoulder-length, dark hair and an olive complexion that would make him attractive to women. He was engaged in small talk with the bartender. Ken ordered a burger with fries and coleslaw with an Amstel and pretended to dial someone on his cell phone.

That night as Bobby Ray drove home, his vision bleared by drink, he saw a car stopped by the side of the road. A tall, slender, dark-haired woman stood beside the car with the trunk open. She hailed him as he drove by.

"Oh, hell," he said, skidding to a stop several feet past the car. *Woman needs help. Who knows, she might be grate-ful.*

He backed the truck up and parked in front of the car.

"Oh, thank you for stopping!" she said. "My car just sputtered and stopped. I don't know what to do. Maybe you can help or give me a ride to town."

"Well, lemme see." He slid behind the steering wheel and turned the key.

He felt the cold muzzle of the gun on the back of his neck.

"Get out very slowly with your hands up," growled Ken.

"Who are you? I ain't got no money, if that's what you want."

"That's not what I want." Ken ordered Bobby Ray into the back seat, handed the gun to Karen, locked the door, then went to the opposite side and slid in beside him. Karen trained the gun on Bobby Ray, while Ken turned on a flashlight. Its beam illuminated a newspaper article with a photo of Grace Patterson and the headline "Murder of Local Teacher Shocks Community."

"What do you know about this murder?"

"I don't know nothin'. I ain't never seen that woman before."

"We have new information about the case and …"

"Are you the police?"

"No, we're not the police ... You might find us scarier than the police. Let me introduce us—Karen and Ken Patterson—Grace Patterson's children."

Bobby Ray said, "I don't know nothin' about her." Then, he sat in sullen silence.

Ken said, "Okay, we'll try something to see if it improves your memory."

He motioned for Karen to get out of the car, then opened the trunk, got a rope, pulled Bobby Ray out, tied his hands behind his back, and jerked him to the ground. Bobby Ray kicked and screamed, but Ken tied his ankles together. Then, the two of them heaved him into the trunk.

Bobby Ray struggled and yelled, "You can't do this!"

"Yes, we can! We can and we are!" Karen yelled back at him.

She thought of her mother—her life so carelessly snuffed out, her body dumped in the trunk—and she ran to the ditch and vomited.

Ken slammed the trunk shut and went to her, putting his arm around her shoulders.

"I know, sis ... I know."

He drove the truck to a wooded area, and Karen followed him in the car.

He parked the truck, got into the car, and they drove away from the countryside onto the highway. To drown out the muffled sounds from the trunk, they tuned the radio to a hard rock station, turned the volume as high as bearable, and drove for about an hour, then pulled off on a secluded road.

They stopped and opened the trunk.

"I'll ask you again, Mr. Baker. What happened the night my mother was murdered?"

"Look, get me out of here. I'll tell you."

They lifted him out of the trunk but didn't untie him.

"I know where you got your information—from Dale Jenkins, my brother-in-law. But I bet he didn't tell you that he was the one who killed her, did he? She yelled at him and he knocked her down and hit her head on concrete. That's how it happened. It wasn't my idea to rob her, but I had to help him put her in the trunk. Now, he wants to get rid of me."

"I don't believe your story, Mr. Baker. I want to see her driver's license and purse. I want you to take us to the place where they're hidden."

"I ain't got them. Honest. Dale's got them. I don't know where he put them."

Ken motioned to Karen, and they lifted him into the trunk.

"*No, no* … don't put me back in here! I can't stand it! Take me out. I'll get them things from Dale and bring them to you, but I can't do it tonight."

"No deal, Baker. You need to think about it some more."

Ken closed the trunk, and, once more, they drove silently, this time fifties' rock filling the space between them to mask sounds coming from the trunk.

After several minutes, Karen said, "I haven't heard any noise for a while. We should check on him again."

When they found a place to stop, Ken went into the bushes to relieve himself. Karen opened the trunk. Bobby Ray was silent. She thought he'd fallen asleep. She shook his arm, but he didn't respond.

"*Ken!*"

"I'm coming."

"Ken, something's wrong."

"Come on, Baker, stop playing 'possum."

Her nurse's training kicking in, Karen felt for his pulse and got none.

"*Ohmygod*, Ken, I think he's dead!"

They placed the body in the bed of the truck. Then, Ken drove the truck, and Karen drove the car. She followed him to a side road that appeared to lead only to a junk yard. There, she parked the car and got into the truck, and Ken drove to what was known locally as Quarry Hill. Actually, it was two moderately steep hills forming the sides of an inverted arc. It was sport for local teenagers to go down one hill too fast to get the roller-coaster thrill of the dip as the car ascended the other hill. There were no guard rails—only some large rocks along the side to deter a plunge into an abandoned rock quarry on either side of the road.

Ken crossed the arc, driving toward town, then turned around and headed back the other way. Halfway down the first hill, he stopped.

"We have to work fast! Help me put him in the driver's seat."

When Bobby Ray's body was in the driver's seat, Ken took off his jacket and used it to wipe the truck free of fingerprints, then used it again to prevent more fingerprints as they pushed the truck down the embankment.

"Ken, I see headlights coming!"

They ran and then rolled into some bushes. The car passed by without incident.

They walked back to Ken's car, hiding once in the ditch to avoid being seen by a passing vehicle.

###

The murder, apparently drug-related, rocked the small, rural community. Its citizens associated such crimes with urban environs, not thinking about the fact that sizeable marijuana harvests needed the countryside to hide and grow.

The local, weekly newspaper reported that Dale Jenkins was found face down with a bullet hole in his chest in the middle of a marijuana patch on the property of his wife, Darla Jenkins, the former Darla Baker. Much of the marijuana appeared to have been harvested recently. Mrs. Jenkins reportedly knew nothing about the marijuana. Dale Jenkins had served a 3-year prison term for drug dealing, but he was trying to go straight. He had promised her that he would not deal in drugs for the sake of their two children, ages 6 and 8, but he was worried about family finances. Mr. Jenkins' death followed closely the death of Mrs. Jenkins' brother, Bobby Ray Baker, who died in a truck accident on Route 14. The coroner reported that Mr. Baker had apparently suffered a stroke while driving, and the truck plunged into the pit of the old gravel quarry.

Darla Jenkins found a plain brown envelope in her mailbox a month after her husband's death. It contained two crisp hundred dollar bills with a note that an anonymous donor wished to help her financially in raising her children. The envelopes came monthly for the next three years. She told no one about the money and used it well to help her children. Eventually, she married a widowed farmer who lived nearby, and they lived an uneventful life together.

Karen Patterson divorced her husband, remarried and had a son by her second husband. Ken never married but was a doting uncle to his niece and nephew. He was also a Big Brother to two boys living with their mothers in single-parent homes. In his work, he fought for environmental justice.

Ten years after the death of Dale Jenkins, Ken was killed in a head-on collision with a van. In a bank safety deposit box, Karen found a handgun and her mother's wallet and driver's license. She disposed of the gun by dropping it into the river but kept her mother's belongings. She told no one about these items, but the scenarios they presented would disturb her thoughts and her sleep for many years to come. ■

The Vigilante

The battered, white van pulled up in front of the school. The driver jumped out, leaving the door hanging open. He wore a black, ankle-length coat and over-sized aviator sunglasses. He jerked the rear door open and began to unload guns. Double-barreled shotguns, automatic rifles, snub-nosed handguns. A gun that looked like one Clint Eastwood used as "Dirty Harry." And then boxes of ammunition. Working quickly and methodically, he laid them out on the ground.

He paused, then chose two handguns and some ammunition and stuffed them into the pockets of his coat. He picked up a rifle and loaded it but left the other guns on the ground. Pivoting military style, he aimed the rifle at Helen for a moment, and then ran in a crazy, loping motion toward the school.

Helen screamed, lurching awake.

Her gaze swept the school and its grounds.

No van. No guns arrayed on the ground. No black-clad, would-be killer. Just Hardy Drive Elementary School, a modest, single-level, structure with several unoccupied cars in the parking lot. The menace evaporated as a plastic bag skittered across the lawn in the March wind and fluttered against the side of the school.

It was the safe, familiar setting where she dropped her grandchildren, Max and Maddie, off that morning.

Fully awake now, Helen reached for a roll of paper towels in the back seat. She daubed at the tepid coffee that had spilled on her coat. She'd dozed off holding the cup between gloved hands. The car had grown cold, and her feet were icy in her worn oxfords.

Last night, she'd had insomnia—afraid that the dream might terrorize her sleep. Then, she'd dozed off in the car this morning when she was supposed to be alert and watchful, and the dream had visited her anyway. She was upset with herself.

She looked at her watch—10:15. She should get home and see if her husband, Frank, needed anything. Frank had fallen while shoveling snow and broken his leg. Now, he was in a cast and grumpy because he was handicapped in his work as an independent construction contractor for a while.

"Kids miss the damn bus *again*?" he'd grumbled, as she started out the door that morning.

One or the other of their parents dropped off Max and Maddie around 7 a.m., and Helen had always hustled them around to be on time to meet the bus. But lately, she'd stopped that. She *wanted* to take them to school. Some days when they caught the bus, she thought of some other excuse—like she had a book due at the library, or they were out of milk, or something—to get out of the house.

The first nightmare had occurred a few weeks ago in the wake of another school shooting—this time in a high school. The dream was the same except she wasn't at the school, so the killer hadn't pointed his gun at her. Instead, he loped directly to the front entrance of the school and began shooting his way in.

The morning after the nightmare, she received a call from the nurse at Hardy Drive Elementary, asking her to pick up Max, who was coughing and feverish.

As she approached the school, she began to feel anxious and shaky. By the time she was in the school office to sign Max out, she could barely respond intelligibly to the plump secretary's pleasantries and concern.

As she turned to leave, Mrs. Henderson, the secretary, said, "Oh, by the way, Mrs. Morris, the next time you come, we may have a new security system in effect. They're going to install an intercom system and the doors will be locked. All visitors will have to identify themselves before we let them in. Just giving you a 'heads up.'"

Helen said, "Oh, that sounds good."

Outside, the nightmare still fresh in her mind, she thought, *But the Newtown killer shot glass out the windows! How the Sam Hill was locking the doors supposed to help if a would- be killer wanted to shoot his way in?*

The next morning, she found herself parked in the back row of the school parking lot on what was to become the first of many vigils. She had a thermos full of coffee and a paper bag that held an orange and a frosted strawberry Pop Tart, the kind that Max and Maddie liked.

Frank and. others wouldn't understand how the nightmare had gripped her, how she needed … *had* to be here between 9 and 10 a.m.—the time it had been for Sandy Hook.

What would she do if a killer showed up? Well, she would dial 911 as fast as she could, and then run toward him, diverting his attention and possibly sacrificing herself—giving the police time to get there.

The boy in the nightmare was the Newtown killer, or some version of him. She'd done Google searches and knew he wore all black, though not a long black coat. That must have come from the Columbine High School shootings.

A disturbed kid with dead eyes. She thought of him as a kid, although he had been 20 years old. She wondered how old he was in that photo that was shown on Wikipedia and everywhere. She avoided saying his name aloud or even to herself. That might make him seem less monstrous. And his mother … *his mother had bought guns and taught him how to use them! And he had killed her with one of them, apparently as she lay sleeping.* She understood that parents sometimes can be blind to their children's problems, but that kid had been flashing abnormality in neon!

Though she wasn't sure why her dream had the would-be killer laying all the guns out on the ground—that just wouldn't happen—she knew things in dreams weren't always realistic. Actions, things sometimes stood for something else— "symbolism" was the word. Maybe, she thought, that act— almost a ritual—symbolized the prevalence of guns. So many people being murdered every day with them.

Though she knew almost nothing about guns, she had memorized the names of the guns the Newtown killer had used—a Bushmaster something, an automatic rifle, and two handguns, a Glock and a Sig Sauer.

Her father had been a hunter and kept his guns in small clothes closet in a spare bedroom that was generally locked. That the guns were there was no secret, but she was warned never to handle them. One day, she found the room unlocked.

Shivering with the excitement of the forbidden, she opened the closet door and just stood staring at the rifle and shotgun she'd seen her father carry. She touched the barrel of the rifle with her index finger, and then quickly drew it back—like she'd touched something hot. The closet was dusky and smelled faintly of oil. The impression was of heaviness and power that she associated with masculine things.

But she'd married a man who did not hunt and had no need for guns.

The driver in the car behind her honked his horn and shook his fist. The light had turned green, and she'd just sat there lost in thought. After she made a left turn, the man sped up and cut sharply in front of her. His bumper sticker read, "You can have my gun when you pry it from my cold, dead fingers."

When she got home, Norm, their neighbor, a retired construction worker was at the kitchen counter, drinking a beer and shooting the shit with Frank. Helen breezed through the kitchen, not bothering to speak to Norm. Going upstairs, she heard Frank say, "She's always running around doing something—doesn't tell me much. A mystery woman." They chuckled. "Ha-ha," she said to herself. She was in no mood to chit-chat with Norm, who was an NRA member and a hunter with an extensive gun collection. Gun people! They were everywhere.

Max and Maddie (for Madison) would come home on the bus about 3:15. Max, age 8, would play games on his Nintendo. Maddie would take over the television and watch her latest TV binge show, "Pawn Stars"—an odd choice for a

10-year-old. But Frank liked the program, too, so it was a bonding time for them.

Who would pick them up this evening? Her son, Jim? Or their mother, Mary Jane? They were separated but trying to be civilized and share childcare. Jim had found out that MJ was having an affair with a co-worker. Helen hated how the separation affected the kids. They were quieter, less sunny. Precocious in some ways, Maddie was turning cynical.

Then, there was her daughter, Sarah, who had been laid off from her job as a computer support specialist at a large IT company. Recently, she'd called, saying that she would maybe need to move back home for a while. She'd broken up with the guy she'd lived with for the last two years and couldn't afford the rent on an apartment of her own. Helen and Frank had given her a small sum of money, and Sarah had found a woman to share an apartment with. She was hanging on, working temp jobs, but she was having trouble keeping up her end of the financial agreement. Helen did not think it would work out for her to move back home. Sarah was 23 and would be resentful because she was beholden to them. She'd indulge in behavior Helen wouldn't approve of, like staying out late drinking with old high school buddies. She'd be slovenly, leaving empty soda cans and items of clothing all over the place. Helen would have to nag her to pick up after herself and to help with the housework. Sara would sulk and grudgingly comply, and Frank would likely excuse her behavior, telling Helen to lay off because Sara was going through a bad period in her life. And, what's more, Sara wouldn't be a good role model for Maddie, who was at an impressionable age and coping with the separation of her parents.

On top of all the family problems, their furnace died in February. Installing a new one had put a considerable dent in their savings, and with Frank being unable to work, they had less income.

Problems, problems!

###

Monday dawned bright and sunny with a pale blue sky. The piercing March wind had abated. There was maybe a whiff of spring in the air.

Helen had rushed out of the house, forgetting her thermos of coffee and bag of snacks, so she decided to indulge herself. After she dropped Max and Maddie off, she went to Tim Horton's drive-thru and ordered a tall coffee with cream and two chocolate, glazed donuts—calories she didn't need, not to mention it was a splurge when she should be saving money. Then, she drove back to the school with the aroma of the guilty treats fueling her alertness for the morning's vigil.

Her anxiety had lessened. She felt wide awake, almost anticipatory.

In the school parking lot, she sipped the strong coffee, ate one of the donuts, and then reached into the glove compartment. Her fingers curved around the unfamiliar grip, just getting the feel of it. Recommended for women, the guy in the shop had told her. He had shown her how to use it—a Glock 19. She'd signed up for more lessons.

She would be ready for him—if he came. ■

1984

The day the new on-line card catalogs arrived in the library marked the beginning of the end of Mrs. Lilah Lamb's 25-year-library career. Or perhaps it was the day Mr. Chesterton, the new director, stepped into the library a year and some months earlier, in January 1984, a year for technological bodings.

Mr. Chesterton was leading the Irving Public Library into the electronic age with the library board's blessing. He even tried to make the transition to automation as painless as possible. To let patrons and staff get used to electronic browsing gradually, he decreed that the computer terminals should be placed on the cabinets that housed the cards. That way, people--he sometimes said Luddites--could test drive the new catalogs but still consult the cards should they be intimidated by the computers. The card catalog ceased to be reliable though because new acquisitions no longer were added to it. The stage had been set for the time when the cards would disappear entirely.

Lilah, Head of the children's library, was herself a Luddite and proud of it. She regarded the machines as invaders, an occupying force ostensibly there to help, but in reality, waiting to perform a coup and usurp power from the rightful ruler, the venerable card catalog. She waged a futile guerilla campaign to save the cards. When patrons began to experiment with the electronic catalogs, she sympathized with their frustrations.

Ms. Mary Hoskins, mild-mannered reference librarian in the adult services division, scolded Lilah and counseled her against careless remarks.

"You mustn't be rash, dear! Give it time."

The two had been housemates and lovers for nearly twenty years. Mary knew well Lilah's strong will and tendency to obsess over matters in the children's library. Two competent assistant librarians had quit because they couldn't tolerate her inflexibility and need to control every detail of management and organization.

A "steel magnolia" from a well-to-do southern family, Lilah had long been a midwesterner, but was aware of the charm of her honeyed accent, using it selectively when it worked to her advantage. The former library director, also a genteel, southern woman, had felt a kinship with Lilah and had given her free rein to administer the children's library.

Lilah's arbitrariness and exactitude did not diminish Mary's affection. In fact, she had a certain fascination with this part of her partner's personality, even as she sympathized with the victims of it.

Professionally, Mary was competent, objective, open-minded, and interested in new technology. She preferred working with adults or older students, and, if the truth be known, would have been better suited to a career in an academic library. She'd long ago given up that aspiration when Lilah persuaded her to apply for the position at Irving Public Library. She was a poet who had a few of her poems published in literary journals.

Lilah had worked with children her entire career. She loved children but also had a mission. She regarded herself as the one of the last bastions in protecting innocent young minds, and she practiced censorship liberally under the guise of responsible collection development. Because Irving was a conservative community, Lilah enjoyed some loyalty and support among mothers. She resisted modern writers of realistic, young adult literature like Judy Blume, transferring their works to the adult fiction section if possible.

The fact that Lilah herself lived an alternative lifestyle that many conservative members of the community might find objectionable was tucked away in a compartment of her mind that she rarely opened. She and Mary had a tacit agreement that they should present themselves as merely companions who shared a house for the purposes of companionship and economy. For Mary, this charade was a pragmatic solution. Perhaps if they'd lived and worked in a broad-minded academic community, she would have been open about the relationship, but she cringed at the thought of being ridiculed in Irving.

Lilah had once been married briefly and had a daughter, Darla, who was now 27 years old and lived in California. Lilah's husband was an alcoholic abuser, who had died in a drunken driving accident two years after the divorce. She'd retained the Mrs. title, not just for the sake of camouflage, but because it was important to her self-image. In fits of pique, she developed a revisionist version of her marriage, speaking of her former husband in, if not glowing, at least adequate terms and assuming a slightly condescending air toward Mary.

For her part, Mary endured these episodes stoically, as she did Darla's vague disapproval of her. Usually, Lilah spent one week of the three weeks' vacation due her visiting Darla. It worked out well. It helped to give them the image of having separate lives and saved Mary from suffering through an awkward visit with Darla and a seaside vacation.

Mary did not share her partner's love of beaches. Too much sun gave her a rash, the smell of coconut oil made her nauseous, and she was self-conscious about her tall, thin, ungainly figure in a bathing suit. She also thought it the height of folly for people to bake themselves in the sun.

Her tastes in vacations ran to browsing the Smithsonian or strolling through Williamsburg, cruising Skyline Drive in its early autumn brilliance, or, best of all, touring the Louvre and European castles. She and Lilah had done all those things. But, still, Lilah had this affinity for the ocean.

On a cool, rainy day in mid-April, Mary sat in a program at the annual state library association conference, staring gloomily out the window thinking there was no way to deny Lilah's plans for a vacation on the beach of North Carolina. She had tried persuading her to spend a week or two in a mountain cabin in North Carolina instead, but Lilah wouldn't hear of it. Darla had "special projects and business trips" which, translated, meant that she had a new man in her life, and Lilah felt she should not impose. Instead, she insisted the two of them would have a nice seaside vacation.

Mary thought about Lilah's difficulties the past few months. She'd remained inflexible in her rejection of the electronic catalog and grieved for the card catalog that had now been removed. On top of that, the hated electronic wonders had exposed her cache of new books that she held to scrutinize for objectionable material before placing them on the shelves. But with the catalogs showing status as "available" once new items had been processed, there had been some patron complaints about not finding these items on the shelf. Mr. Chesterton caught on and told Lilah that keeping books out of circulation was simply unacceptable.

With so many stresses, Lilah could not be denied. And so, in North Carolina, on a balmy July evening, Mary found herself strolling the beach with Lilah when they came upon a group of students partying in the glow of a bonfire. Rolling Stones' music pulsated from a boom box, competing with the roar of the surf. Grinding his hips and snapping his fingers, a skinny guy with shoulder-length hair gave a wolf whistle and pretended to leer at them.

"Hey mamas, wanna dance?"

Mary stared straight ahead rigidly, but moments later, she became aware that Lilah had slipped from her side and stepped into the circle of light.   Mary watched in disbelief as her partner began gyrating her apple-shaped body. Lilah—her bulges ill-concealed by a loose multicolored, terrycloth wrap over a fuchsia bathing suit— moved with a peculiar grace.

The group, stunned by the unexpected brazenness of this plump, middle-aged stranger, wavered between derision and embarrassment. But abruptly, as though simultaneously affected by an ocean breeze, they relaxed and began clapping and laughing in approval. Lilah was a high priestess who joined the natives in a ritual.

After a few seconds, she stepped blithely out of the circle, gave a mocking curtsy and rejoined Mary in their stroll. The boy who had first called out hurried after them. Mary feared harassment, but he just laughed drunkenly and pressed icy Budweisers into their hands. He called Lilah a "cool old lady" and, still laughing, returned to the party.

Later, Lilah lightly dismissed the incident. It was just a silly thing she felt like doing, she said, and she refused to talk about it anymore.

Mary was left to dwell in silence on its meaning, to try to reconcile the writhing creature in firelight with the censorious mate she lived with in Irving. The incident both intrigued and unsettled her. It gave her partner a dimension that she could not fathom, a mysterious, exotic quality. Trying to capture the moment in poetry, she gravitated toward images of primitive, tribal rituals—voodoo and witchcraft. Mary regarded superstition as a weakness of the intellect but, nevertheless, could not shake the feeling that a spell had been cast.

A month passed, and Lilah seemed in good spirits at work. Mary decided that her misgivings were the product of an overwrought poetic imagination. Then, Mr. Chesterton called Lilah into his office and asked why there had been no progress in getting the backlog of books into circulation. To which Lilah replied that she'd just been too busy since returning from two weeks' vacation. To which Mr. Chesterton replied that, yes, he realized she'd been gone on vacation, but this project was a priority with him. In a dictatorial tone, he stated that she should set aside some time each morning and get it done in two weeks. Lilah summoned all the dignity her bulk would allow and marched out.

At mid-morning break, Mary found her in amid her basement cache, vigorously slamming books from one set of shelves to another three feet away.

"That man," shrilled Lilah, "doesn't know ..." But Mary quickly signaled caution with a raised finger, as a technical services staff member entered the room. Then, she talked quietly for several minutes trying to soothe Lilah.

That afternoon, Lilah dropped into her desk chair for a breather from the after-school rush. As she sat surveying the room, she had an inexplicable mental nudge. Something wasn't quite right. The orange blink of the cursor on the computer monitor seemed to signal her. Above it, she saw the bold words: "F___ you, Mrs. Lambchop!"

Sharply, she surveyed the room, her eyes resting on an angelic, blond boy, sitting cross-legged in a corner of the fiction section. No, it couldn't have been Alan! His mother had been bringing him to the library since he was a toddler. Now, he was eight years old and cocky, losing some of his innocent charms, but still respectful, often stopping at the desk to talk about his new baby sister or his dog, Bruno. But wait, he was leaning forward and laughing. Who was he with? She rose from her chair and walked to the end of the room opposite Alan, choosing a place where she could observe him without his seeing her. From her vantage point, she could see that he was with Jimmy, a noisy, impudent boy. Now, Jimmy was peering around the end of a row of shelves, looking directly at her desk and giggling. She gripped the new fiction display, struggling for control. She wanted to shake Jimmy's shoulders until he lost his smirk. For a second, she teetered on the brink of irrationality.

When she was past the point of overreacting, she moved to a point closer to the boys. Jimmy laughed, then noticed her, rolling his eyes and slapping his hand over his mouth. She glared at him with an intensity that could have curled the pages of the book he was pretending to read. He shoved the book into the stacks and hightailed it to the exit.

Shaken, she walked unsteadily back to her desk and dialed Mary, demanding that she come to the children's library. Mary sighed and made an excuse to step down to the children's section.

"Look! Just look!" Lilah demanded, swiveling the monitor so that Mary could see.

Looking at the screen, Mary was almost relieved to find that the situation had nothing to do with Mr. Chesterton. She summoned her best "What-is-the-younger-generation-coming-to?" attitude and said, "Oh Lilah, children today, I just don't know... Please try not to let it upset you so much." Then, with the efficiency she applied to reference transactions, she reached over the desk, pulled the keyboard toward her, pressed the "Screen print" key, ripped the printout neatly from the printer, then deleted the offending message.

Dropping the printout into her skirt pocket, she said, "Lilah, you're shaking. It's been too much for you! Why don't you say you don't feel well? Go to the office and relax until 6 o'clock? Please! I have to go back to desk duty now."

The next morning Mary made breakfast as usual. When the smell of bacon and eggs didn't bring Lilah to the kitchen, Mary climbed the stairs to check on her. She shook her gently. "Time to rise and shine," she said brightly.

Peering over the edge of a multicolored quilt, Lilah appeared disoriented at first. Then, she rolled over on her side away from Mary's probing eyes, and said decisively, "Can't go in today!"

"What's wrong, Lilah? Is it yesterday's incident? Are you really sick?"

"Sick, sick! Yes, sick. Tell Mr. Know-it-all I'm sick!" She jerked the cover over her head.

"Okay. I'm sure it'll be okay. There are no special programs today. And you're so seldom sick."

She sat on the bed a few moments, then patted Lilah's shoulder, and said "I'll call at noon to see how you're doing."

At lunch time, Mary took her ham sandwich and apple to the staff lounge. She wanted to call Lilah from there, but Alicia, another reference librarian, was chatting over the phone, presumably to her husband, a burly truck driver who was on the road a lot. Alicia was a redheaded, hippy woman of ample, though not obese, proportions, with cunning eyes and a snide sense of humor.

There was to be no privacy in the staff lounge, so she went to the lobby to use a pay phone. Lilah answered after several rings, and, in a voice that lacked inflection, said that she was okay. In the background, Mary could hear a soap opera theme song. She decided that Lilah was in a self-pitying mood. She was thankful it was Friday. That would give her the weekend to work it through.

###

On Monday morning—contrary to Mary's hopes—Lilah ignored the 6:30 a.m. alarm, murmuring that she did not feel well enough to go to work yet.

The same thing happened the next two days. On Thursday, when she again rolled over and put her pillow over her head when the alarm buzzed, Mary could no longer keep quiet.

"Lilah, what is wrong? If you're sick, then you need to go see Dr. Henderson!"

"No, I don't want to see Dr. Henderson! I just need rest."

"Okay, Lilah, okay," she sighed. Once again, she would have to go to Mr. Chesterton's office and report that Lilah would not be in. Lilah simply refused to take responsibility for calling in herself.

On Friday evening, Lilah, who had been quieter than usual, began to chatter about the soap operas she'd been watching. Who was having an affair with whom? Who was scheming to break up whose marriage on *Days of Our Lives* or *As the World Turns*? Mary had nothing but disdain for soap operas. Soon, she tuned out all the details and observed her mate with equal parts astonishment and alarm. What was happening to her?

After Lilah talked herself out, she was again quieter than usual, and the weekend passed quietly with Lilah spending a lot of time in front of the television and Mary retreating to the spare bedroom that functioned as an office. Sunday evening, as they shared a nightcap, Mary decided to take a more assertive approach.

"You've really got to return to work, Lilah. I hate to see you sitting home all day watching soaps. It's just not right!"

Lilah turned her head slightly and stared into space. Several minutes passed with no response.

"Well?" Mary said.

"Hah-wah-yeh!" Lilah said exaggeratedly, in a voice that wafted the scent of magnolias. "I want to go to Hah-wah-yeh."

"Hawaii! Lilah, we've already had our vacation this year in North Carolina."

"Not a vacation." Lilah waved one arm expansively. "I want to LIVE in Hah-wah-yeh!"

"Live in Hawaii? Lilah, that's just silly!" Mary gulped the rest of her sherry.

"Lilah, you need to think really hard about pulling yourself together in the next few days." She paused. "Please, Lilah, you know I'm right. Why don't you come to bed now? Get a good night's rest."

When the alarm sounded the next morning, Mary didn't even try to coax Lilah out of bed. She felt helpless and dreaded the day.

Mary hoped to be able to report to Mr. Chesterton's secretary and avoid the director himself. But as soon as she turned around, he materialized in the doorway. Mr. Chesterton was a man in his middle forties with an aquiline nose and a direct gaze that made him appear slightly ferocious when he was serious. The extra 15-20 pounds he carried on his medium frame added to his air of intimidation. When in a good humor, he was witty and charming. But today he stood unsmiling in the doorway, making it impossible for her to pass.

"Good morning, Mary!" he boomed.

"Good morning," she replied, hating the edge of shrillness she heard in her voice.

She tried to appear preoccupied and businesslike.

"Is Lilah still sick?" he asked, with a slight emphasis on the "still."

"Yes, yes, I'm afraid so."

"Mary, what is wrong with Lilah exactly?"

"Well, she's having, uh, headaches … and some dizziness, I believe. Yes, she's complained of being dizzy."

"Has she been to a doctor?"

"Well, er … I think she has an appointment."

"Good. Good."

"Mary, I know it's logical for you to report in for Lilah, but it's not really your problem, now, is it?"

"This is what?" he continued. "The seventh day that Lilah's been out, and she hasn't called me at all. I want to hear from Lilah personally, if she is able to call me. I need to talk to her about staffing. I expect Lilah to call me if she's going to be out tomorrow."

"Yes, of course. I'll tell her." Mary felt reprimanded.

"Tell you what, Mary. I think I'll call Lilah today myself. Do you know when a good time might be?"

"Well—maybe late morning, between 11 and 12."

She went directly to a telephone and called Lilah to warn her, wondering as she did so, if that's what Mr. Chesterton expected her to do. She'd always gotten along well with him, felt there was a mutual professional respect, but she resented him for making her squirm, no matter if her intellect told her his expectations were fair and reasonably stated.

Despite Mary's trepidations, his talk with Lilah apparently went well enough, and she agreed to his request for a doctor's statement if she did not return to work the following week.

"Then you'll go see Dr. Henderson?" Mary asked that evening.

"Ah guess."

"I'll make the appointment tomorrow then."

Dr. Henderson had been their physician for only three years, but Mary trusted her. She specialized in internal medicine but also functioned as their general practitioner. Mary explained about Lilah's work absence and indicated that she had been under some stress.

"Have there been any other unusual behaviors, Mary?"

Mary thought of the beach incident, but then dismissed it. "No, other than a lot of television watching, I can't think of anything. Well—this probably doesn't mean much, but she insists she wants to go live in Hawaii."

Dr. Henderson chuckled. "That sounds like a fantasy many of us have when we're weighed down by everyday matters. It may be that this is a temporary episode brought on by work stress. I'll need to do a thorough examination to rule out any underlying physical problems. I'll see her on Tuesday."

###

After giving Lilah a thorough physical exam, Dr. Henderson reported a slightly elevated blood pressure, high cholesterol, and fatigue, possibly of viral origin. She gave Lilah a written statement, prescribing an indeterminate period of rest, and Mary felt some relief.

In the evenings though, "I want to live in Hah-wah-yeh" now became a refrain. If Mary hadn't begun to feel like she was camped on the slope of a rumbling volcano, she would have found the subject of Hawaii more boring than the tedious first chapter of Michener's novel.

Mary countered with arguments about premature retirement, gawking, boorish tourists, the lack of variation in seasons, and, above all, the high cost of living.

Mary came home from work one day to find Lilah absent. She had left a note clipped to a manila envelope lying on the kitchen table. The message, "MARY LOOK AT THIS," was printed in large, bold letters. The envelope contained a bank statement and other financial records. All of it added up to several hundred thousand dollars in Lilah's name.

Mary sat at the kitchen table, holding her forehead, half in shock.

"Oh Lord!" she muttered.

She knew that Lilah had inherited some money from her parents, but she'd never asked how much, and Lilah hadn't volunteered. She thought that Lilah probably had given a large amount to Darla for travel and the purchase of a condo. She had no idea…That evening, Lilah did not mention Hawaii, nor did she refer to the financial records. She sat with a self-satisfied, half-smile, magnanimous in her perceived victory. Mary had a pinched look and could not hide her discomposure. Her unspoken words were as prominent to her as a billboard message: *I don't want to live in Hawaii, no matter how much money you have!* But she was unable to say them aloud.

A few days after Lilah was officially put on medical leave, Mr. Chesterton announced the appointment of Ms. Deborah Whiteside as a temporary librarian in the children's division. He had not discussed the decision to hire Ms. Whiteside with Lilah beforehand but called her that day to inform her of his decision.

At noon hour, Mary walked into the small kitchen just off the staff lounge, removed her macaroni and cheese from the refrigerator, and put it in the microwave. She could hear Alicia, her coworker, talking lowly in confidence. She tried not to listen, but Alicia's voice rose, as she dramatized with comic zest. "She's a dinosaur…"

Alicia was talking to Ms. Whiteside, Lilah's temporary replacement. Then, abruptly, the conversation ended. Intuitively, Mary knew the subject of conversation had changed due to her presence. Ms. Whiteside blushed and looked discomfited. Alicia pretended to be amused by a magazine article. Her cover-up was transparent.

Mary ate lunch hurriedly and escaped to the bathroom to regain her poise. Her face burned. The scales had fallen from her eyes. She had thought that Lilah's foibles, if not altogether unnoticed, were mostly ignored by the library staff.

Mary functioned robotically the rest of the day and faced the evening uneasily. Would she find a talkative Lilah? A depressed Lilah? A Lilah packing her bags for Hawaii? It seemed too much to hope for a Lilah jarred to her senses and ready to return to work.

What she found was a "made over" Lilah who provided possibilities but no answers. She was sitting on the living room couch waiting to be noticed. Her graying, light brown hair had been permed and dyed orange with henna. Her cheeks were two coral patches of rouge, her eyes were smeared with black mascara, and her nails were red and glossy. Instead of her usual, loose caftan, she wore a purple, polyester blouse with a black skirt and pumps. She smiled seductively.

"Well, what do you think?"

"What do I think? I thought we had a visitor!"

"Don't you like it?" She patted her hair.

"Well, well, let me see." Mary walked around her, with an exaggerated leer, one hand cupping her chin, the other on her hip. Lilah giggled, and Mary knew that she was in her cups.

"You look lovely!" she half-lied—"lovely" intoxicating her tongue like hot-buttered rum. She remembered an English tour guide who seemed to use the word in every other sentence. Actually, she thought the hair color and makeup were garish, but the perm style was nice, and it was good to see Lilah dressed in something besides her usual muumuu and pink fuzzy house slippers.

Mary suddenly felt quite happy, realizing that it had been much too long since they had been playful.

They ordered a pizza and downed a six-pack of beer with it. They put on Glenn Miller records and danced slow dances and a couple of silly swings, giggling and giving in to the mood.

At one point, Lilah turned solemn and pronounced, "She can have it!"

"Who can have what, dear?"

"She—Miss Blackside! She can have it—the computers, the books—*the whole she-bang*!"

"Oh, Lilah … this will pass. You've been feeling down, but this will pass. Just try to be positive."

###

Shortly after lunch the next day, Mary was checking on an interlibrary loan request in the backroom of the circulation department. She became aware of a flurry of attention among the circulation staff as they greeted someone they'd apparently not seen for a while. Their voices were effusive, well-meaning, and not altogether sincere.

"Oh, my goodness. Nice to see you!"

"Your hair looks so-oh nice!"

Mary stepped to the doorway and saw Lilah, blinking, half smiling, but looking a little surprised, as though she had forgotten about her changed appearance. She wore the now rumpled blouse and skirt she'd worn last evening. The rouge was gone, but she had dusted her puffy face with a light powder that made her face look floury. It was the first time during her leave that Mary felt she really looked ill.

Mary stepped from behind the circulation desk and started toward Lilah. Involuntarily, she paused, her eyes riveted on Lilah's feet. Lilah looked at her, looked down, and then back at Mary in alarm. Instead of the black pumps, she wore the fuzzy pink slippers.

The three women who had gathered at the circulation desk were a tableau of embarrassment.

Mary took Lilah gently by the arm, and said, "Oh dear, Lilah, you shouldn't have tried to come. I don't think you're feeling up to it."

"Oh yes, you look a little pale!" one lady chimed in. Another aborted a nervous giggle.

Mary guided Lilah through the door and to the parking lot. She thought she would get Lilah seated in the car, then go back and tell her supervisor that she needed time to drive her home. At the car though, Lilah began to sob and turned to cling to Mary. She was strong and grasping, pulling Mary's face toward hers. Mary struggled to turn her head, Lilah's kiss brushing the corners of her mouth.

"Teach me … teach me everything you know … about the computers," Lilah murmured.

Mary stood paralyzed, locked in Lilah's embrace. Over her shoulder, she caught sight of Alicia and a friend returning from lunch. They both stared. A gleam of derision flashed across Alicia's face, followed by a sly smile.

Images of the future washed over Mary like surly ocean breakers. There would be stifled laughter and hushed voices when she entered rooms. There would be innuendo and speculation and crude jokes. The library grapevine would eventually grow and creep insidiously into the community. There might be complaints--

Then, she grew decisively calm. She saw herself, walking on an empty beach in the early morning, Prufrock-like, with trousers rolled, a resigned set to her shoulders. She watched as her back receded into the distance and disappeared into the ocean mist. ∎

A Sunday Afternoon

"**M**ike, I baked a blackberry cobbler just for you. Your dad told me it's your favorite," said Margaret, my new stepmother, placing a bakery-perfect pie on the table.

She put a large helping on a plate and set it in front of my brother.

"Yeah, thanks," he mutters, taking one bite, then turning to my dad to engage him in a spirited harangue about how Ohio State would win the game with Michigan in the fall. It's their thing, the good-natured rivalry. We live in Michigan, and Mike is now at Ohio State. All the while he talks to Dad, Mike nurses his coffee and plays with his pie like a 3-year-old. I am embarrassed for Margaret and both a little ashamed of and amused at Mike.

A part of me would like to be able to express my resentment of Margaret, even if in a childish way. For my entire life though, I've always been the peacemaker, the oldest child, always seeing both sides of an issue and mediating between parties. It's a quality that has served me well. In high school, I was nominated to attend a summer camp on leadership, and now, I supervise 20 employees in the education and training division of a large computer company. But there are times when I just plain get tired of being so responsible.

None of us expected Dad to remarry at sixty-two. We never even entertained the idea that he might need a woman in his life. My other siblings, Judith and Ken—the ones between Mike and me—are married with two children each. Dad is a wonderful grandfather, roughhousing with them and keeping two ponies for them to ride when they visit. We thought we were enough for him

What's more, if he had to get married, why did he have to marry someone so different from Mom? And from me, I might add? I have a sizeable infrastructure, you might say. I'm 5'10" and large-boned with dark-brown hair, just like Mom, except Mom carried about 30 extra pounds that she always covered with tent-like dresses. Margaret is 5'4", slender, and—thanks to Clairol— still blond even though she's two years older than Dad. Of course, my ever-well-functioning, inner critic immediately jumps to her defense, saying, "Now, Emma, that was catty. Don't make her sound like a blond floozy! She's not."

No, she's certainly not. In fact, she's far too perfect. She has a warm personality and looks ten years younger than her age. Moreover, she possesses none of Mom's extravagances. Margaret is tactful, soft-spoken, neat, and frugal; Mom was noisy, opinionated, disorganized, and generous to a fault. The thing is, it makes me wonder if Dad was happy with Mom all those years.

The thought of Mom's death six years ago still brings a stab of pain to my gut. She'd survived the milestone fifth year after treatment for breast cancer and thought she'd beat it. Then, she started having dizzy spells and brief blackouts. The cancer had metastasized to her brain. Months of agony and heartbreak followed. She refused to believe that she would die.

Denial turned to bitterness. God had failed her. Dad thought she may have found some peace at the end, but I'm not so sure of that.

One of the ways in which Margaret is like Mom is that she is a devoted Catholic, or rather like Mom was before she knew she was going to die. That—and she's also a good cook—and she's spent most of her days in this small farm community.

Margaret is the type of person Grandma Anna must have wished Dad had married the first time. Tensions between Mom and "The Anna," as we sometimes referred to her, waxed and waned over the years. Mom always said "The Anna" thought she was the wrong wife for Dad, who Grandma had wanted to become a Methodist minister. "The Anna" was a tall, angular woman--orderly, inflexible, and Methodist. Except for being Catholic, Margaret would have been her ideal daughter-in-law. Still, I know this line of thinking is unfair to Grandma. I remember her sober, stricken appearance when Mom fell ill. I thought then that she regretted their long standoff. Six months after Mom's death, Grandma Anna had died of a heart attack.

Now, Margaret brings the lunch to an end by clearing the dishes from the table. With an air of efficiency, she quietly removes Mike's pie mess while he's still waving his fork in the air.

Dad has a special light in his eye; he announces that he has a surprise for us. Later, he wants us to take a short ride with him, a mile or so down the road. I help Margaret with the dishes while Dad and Mike watch golf distractedly, still talking football. She makes small talk about her children and grandchildren. She has four of each. Her husband died of congestive heart failure two years before Mom died.

When we finish, everything is clean and shipshape, the way the rest of her house is. She and Dad are living in her small, tidy house, so different from the big, rambling farmhouse where I grew up and where Mom and Dad lived their entire married life. Dad is a tall, slender man, who seems a little awkward here. But why shouldn't they live here? Dad is no longer a farmer. And I don't think any of us would want to see Margaret in the old house.

The old house where things were ever chaotic! There were usually dirty dishes in the sink, and the counters overflowed with flotsam and jetsam. Mom was usually available to help us with our 4-H projects, but she neglected the house. Housekeeping was the least of her priorities. We kids were supposed to clean on Saturdays, but we usually did a half-assed job of it. We'd sensed her lack of interest and knew we could do just enough to get by.

In her mid-forties, Mom started a small crafts business with her best friend, Leona. Leona was a talented seamstress. Mom came up with creative ideas and did just about everything else that needed to be done. She wrapped, taped, pasted, painted, and stuffed. She cut out patterns, arranged displays, and kept the books. Mostly, their business concentrated on seasonal holiday projects—4th of July banners, Thanksgiving centerpieces, Halloween costumes, and Christmas wreaths and ornaments—but anything that caught their fancies and they thought might sell was considered. A spare bedroom was devoted to their activities, but the clutter—shreds of fabrics, colored markers, bottles of glue, scissors, DIY books, etc.—always spilled out into the living room where they worked and watched the soaps together in the afternoon.

After three years, the rheumatoid arthritis in Leona's hands began to bother her so much that she found it difficult to sew, and the business foundered. What Mom had liked best about the business was marketing and contact with people. She found a more-than-suitable new outlet for her skills. She ran for and was elected to the county board of commissioners. In that position, she spent hours and hours meeting and talking on the telephone with constituents and other people.

Quick-tempered, Mom never held back when she was unhappy with Dad or us kids. She yelled at us and then hugged us, and we were used to it. We just disappeared until the brief storms were over. She ardently defended us, even when she shouldn't have. When Mike's fifth grade teacher had the audacity to say that Mike needed more discipline in his studies, Mom said Mike was doing just fine; he just needed to be a regular boy until he got around to applying himself. He was her baby and could do no wrong. In college now, he's still undisciplined.

Now, we are on our way to see Dad's little surprise. It's only a short distance from the old farm, he says. Dad is driving his van; Mike is sitting in front with him. Margaret and I are in the back. We turn down a gravel road and go about a quarter of a mile.

This is land that Dad purchased some time ago. He built a small barn on it and keeps his two ponies in the pasture. We turn into the driveway to the barn, and to the right, I see a foundation is being constructed for another building. He stops the car and points to the construction.

"This is going to be Margaret's and my new home," he announces proudly.

My face feels rubbery, but I make a great effort to be polite while we get the guided tour of the home-to-be. It will be two stories, with a two-car garage. On the ground floor, they will have a great room, a master bedroom, kitchen, and a nice laundry room with storage space, especially for Margaret. On the second floor, there will be bedrooms and a play area for grandchildren.

Mike appears interested, asking Dad and Margaret questions, even making suggestions of his own, perhaps trying to make up for his earlier rudeness.

I wander over to the fence and try to get Jack the pony to come to me. He knows I have nothing to feed him, and he's not interested in indulging me. I lean on the fence, trying not to visualize the perfect, neat home that will be created here.

Dad comes over and stands beside me. He puts his arm around my shoulders, and says, "It'll be all right, Emma. Mom, you know, would have wanted …"

But I don't want to listen. I slip from under his arm, spin, and walk away. Fierce tears stinging my eyes, I find myself on the road, striding determinedly toward the house where I grew up.

"Not my mother!" I say to the wind. "Not my mother!" ◾

Apple Blossoms

Just at the edge of consciousness, Martin Johnston thought he had died. He could hear the murmur of voices, but it seemed natural to him to be able to hear after death. To hear but not to understand. He had no desire to understand. A distant hum, not unpleasant, seemed ethereal. He felt peaceful and transcendent.

Then he coughed and became aware of his own voice and the presence of his wife and daughter, standing near the end of his bed. The hum became a throbbing clack as a power mower passed near his bedroom window.

His daughter, Janet, was talking to him, gently coaxing him to do something. He understood the tone but not the request. If he opened his eyes, he felt he would understand her, but he resisted. He wished that she hadn't noticed him stirring. He needed more time to prepare himself for the day's pretenses.

"Lawn … breeze."

What was it she wanted from him?

"Spring is your favorite season, Dad, and it's a gorgeous day."

It came to him like the solution to a crossword clue. She wanted to take him outside.

He started to protest, but went into a coughing spasm, spitting up phlegm instead of irritation.

She had been trying to get him to do things ever since she arrived two days ago. Eat food that nauseated him. Watch television programs that no longer interested him. Walk with the walker when he felt too weak.

Mostly, he wanted to be left alone in the dark coolness of the bedroom with the drawn, blue damask drapes. Once, he had told her the only movement he wanted to make was when the rented hospital bed was adjusted up or down.

Though not ungrateful for the attentions of his wife, Mary, he ignored her frequent questions most of the time. Did he feel better today? Was he comfortable? Did he want a codeine tablet? She ignored his ignoring and continued to ask questions.

Mildly arthritic herself, she had managed to take care of him at home the past few weeks. A visiting nurse came an hour or two each week, and now, Janet and her family had come from Massachusetts for an extended visit. His wife was slow and patient. His daughter, though not exactly impatient, was strong-willed, persistent, always moving, organizing, trying to improve and repair. When she sat on the side of his bed, he could feel the tension in her.

His favorite memory of her was as a preteen, a slightly overweight tomboy with freckles and sandy brown hair, pushed back and rarely parted straight, clothes thrown on without thought and usually disheveled. Now, she was slender, her hair always styled, and her clothes neat and "color-coordinated." She had become an elementary school teacher. A carpenter himself, self-taught in history and literature, he was proud of his daughter's achievements, but wished that she was more relaxed and less preoccupied with organizing people.

Now, she was beside him, touching his arm slightly, but, nonetheless, drawing him out of bed against his will.

He twitched his nose and lips to the right, a slight, characteristic movement that expressed irritation or disapproval.

"Dad, won't you try? We'd love to have you join us."

He wanted to protest, but, instead, found himself sitting, and then standing by the side of his bed, being helped by John, his tall, muscular son-in-law, who was sweaty from mowing the lawn.

Embarrassed by his shrunken body, Martin summoned his strength, drew himself up to his full height and clasped his walker, insisting, "I'll do it!" He managed—with help opening the door and going down the porch steps.

Outdoors, the brightness and greenness overwhelmed him. The smell of newly mown grass filled his nostrils making him dizzy.

With the aid of his walker, he stood, blinking uncertainly. With a light robe over his striped pajamas, he felt like a convict herded into a heavily guarded, recreation area.

Resting between steps, he made his way to the patch of garden recently planted by his wife.

Janet followed solicitously, pleased that he was taking an interest in the garden. His wife and son-in-law trailed a short distance behind.

Ben, the hound, loped goofily over to him, prancing around the walker.

"Look, Dad, he's grinning at you," said Janet. The family had long ago decided that Ben grinned when greeting them.

"Ho, Ben." Martin managed to reach down and pat his head. Ben, who appeared a little lopsided because of an inky blot that spilled across one eye and his nose, planted himself beside Martin, looking up occasionally as though expecting him to say more.

Martin gazed at the garden that was about one-quarter its usual size and toward the pasture at the fishpond he'd had dug five years ago. By the garden fence, the apple tree he thought he might lose last year was in radiant, white bloom.

The breeze touched his body like his wife's gentle hands. Last summer, he had paid close attention to breezes. He had planted the garden, and then sat most of the summer, moving his wooden rocker around the yard to capture the best shade and breeze.

Mary had hoed and harvested and worried while he sat in the chair. She had brought him corn to shuck, peas to hull, and beans to snap. He had started to dig potatoes once but stopped short. He told Mary they looked blighted. The cool, wet weather in the early, growing season probably caused it. At first, she didn't believe him. Exasperated, she dug them herself. But he had been right. They showed the dry rot of blight when exposed to the air.

He did the crossword puzzle in the daily *Sun-Times*, and, once in a while, read a chapter or two in the Civil War books Mary brought from the library. Mostly though, he had sought out breezes and lost himself in the color and sounds around him.

Missouri outdoors, he had once told Janet, was his Boston Pops. The wind did its imitation of violins as it rustled the leaves. Birds were flutes and oboes. Bullfrogs, bass strings. What crickets, bees, and woodpeckers represented, he wasn't sure, but they were a part of the daily, continuous concert. Sometimes, these behind-the-scene musicians played solos with accompaniment; sometimes, they sounded like a full orchestra.

Closing his eyes, now Martin could hear a sparrow's whistling song that ended with a trill.

He remembered last summer as a kaleidoscope image of blue and green, with a few bright, flower-and-vegetable colors, all suffused with sunlight. Turn slightly and there would appear the blacks and grays of evening illuminated by the moon and stars.

During those long, idle days, he had blamed the heat for his lethargy and the pollen for his slight, dry cough.

Summer passed, November came, and the cough deepened and wracked his body. By the New Year, he knew the 25-year cigarette habit he had broken a year ago had gotten him anyway.

A shout from his 5-year-old granddaughter, Susan, startled him back to the present.

"A giant turtle is on the road!" she exclaimed. "We've got to help get him off before he gets run over."

Immediately, Janet ran in the house and came out with a broom.

Mary said, "Let's go see, Martin. Are you up to it?"

She helped him walk to the side of the front porch where they could see the incident.

Janet was trying to shoo the turtle off the road with the broom. The turtle had probably come from their pond and decided to visit the neighbor's pond across the road. Instead of retreating into its shell, the turtle was turning his ugly head and snapping at Janet.

Now, Ben jumped in, springing back and forth and barking at the turtle.

The turtle had accomplished almost two-thirds of its journey across the road before Janet intervened to hurry it along. Now, it seemed to be moving back toward the center instead of going off the road.

Martin started to shake. He was becoming angry.

"Tell her," he said to his wife, "tell her to leave the terrapin alone! Let it find its own way!"

"She's just trying to help."

"I don't care. Tell her to stop!"

Mary saw that he was shaking and patted his arm to reassure him. She called to Janet to stop.

Susan started crying, and her parents comforted her. A car came by, but the driver saw the turtle and swerved. Susan refused to move from her spot near the road. It was as though she felt she could will the turtle to be safe by her presence.

"Too much excitement," said Mary. "Are you ready to go in now, Marty?"

He nodded.

Later, Janet came in and whispered to him that the terrapin made it across the road okay. He didn't open his eyes or reply, but his lips curved in what could have been a half smile.

Martin drifted into sleep. He dreamed about looking out over his land. In his dreamscape, everything appeared as it had when he looked at it earlier, except that the blossoms on the apple tree had become snow. The snow sparkled and blanketed the tree in the sunlight, while birds sang and darted among the leaves in other trees. Snow that didn't melt on a warm, spring day didn't seem strange to him at all. ∎

Four Years

The home health aide called again, saying she would be late. She'd had to take her asthmatic grandson to the emergency room. If it turned out that she couldn't get there soon, the agency she worked for would send a replacement aide.

Nora was upset, saying the aide was unreliable. This was the second time this month she'd had problems She wanted to tell the agency that they needed a different helper, someone they could depend on—no ifs, ands, or buts.

Julia tried to talk her down. "Nora, May's a good woman with a lot on her plate. I don't want her to get any bad marks or, worse yet, get fired. I like her. I've got my Lifeline, and I'll be okay until the other person comes."

Julia could hear Nora's crisp, urgent tone when she called the agency. She managed to keep her irritation in check, just barely, and didn't complain about May in particular, though she made it clear that she needed reliable help.

Julia liked May, a simple woman with a big heart. She was warm and caring, not as cool and clinical as some she'd encountered. It was true that she was beset by family problems that sometimes interfered with her work, but, in Julia's mind, she was desperately juggling responsibilities, trying to do the best she could. She was separated from an alcoholic husband and dealing with a son addicted to crack cocaine and a daughter who had three children, a job that didn't pay enough, and an unemployed husband. Julia lent a willing, sympathetic ear to May's accounts of her messy life. The stories took her out of herself and her health problems. They also made her less lonely, but, of course, she couldn't say that to Nora.

Nora wanted her to be contented and feel well-cared for. And she did feel well-cared for. Contentment was another matter—a complex issue for a 72-year-old woman who'd undergone heart surgery a year ago.

Nora said maybe she should call her supervisor and ask if a substitute could take over her classroom for the morning. Julia's response was an emphatic no. "Please go and live your life and do what you must do. I'll be fine. Just like I used to be in my apartment in Denton."

When Nora finally left, Julia felt like she had pushed her out the door, even though she'd sat in her recliner during the entire stir. Now she could ease into some calm moments before May or whoever arrived. Maybe sensing that she was alone, Tiger the cat strolled in and jumped on her lap adding his welcome purr to the peacefulness.

###

After the surgery, she left her tiny apartment in the small town of Denton and came to live with Nora and John, her daughter and son-in-law, in a city with a population of nearly a million people. Her new home was a "mother-in-law suite," a medium-sized room with attached bath.

When she first moved to this house, she'd sat in her room depressed, feeling like a prisoner. She missed living independently in her small apartment. She'd lost interest in the soap operas she had watched for so many years, and it seemed that every time she turned on TV, all she heard was the scandal about Bill Clinton—a man she had once admired—and Monica Lewinsky.

She thought of her granddaughter Susie who had died in a car accident, the victim of a drunk driver, at age twenty-one. Susie, so young and good-natured, a beacon for all who knew her, not allowed to live her life—to marry and have children or be whatever she wanted to be. And here she was at 71, still alive. She'd had a quadruple heart bypass. It was either that or die shortly, the doctor said. Now, she sometimes wished that she had been brave enough to make the latter choice. Her husband Porter had died at 65 refusing any treatment to extend his life after he'd been diagnosed with colon cancer, but, at 71, she had opted for a dangerous, expensive procedure to prolong her life.

She had become one of her daughter's projects. She was taking 20 mg. of Prozac, had a stack of library books that she had not yet touched, and cable TV with more channels than she'd ever want to watch and a larger screen than anybody needed. She was enthroned in a comfortable recliner, wore a Lifeline monitor on her wrist, and had a bell to ring when she needed something from the family. She had a thermos of cold water, packages of snacks, and the television remote on the table by her chair.

It was an hour before the substitute aide arrived. That hour of solitude had been like oxygen to Julia. She wished there could be more times when she was left alone, but she knew it would not be permitted. That she liked being alone was her secret, and it made her feel good to have a secret. Sometimes, she thought that what she hated most about being old and ill was that it seemed all privacy got stripped away. And people didn't think you were interesting enough to have new secrets. The only escape was thinking about past secrets.

This was the biggest house she'd ever lived in, and when she was alone, she felt a kind of ownership. She felt that she once again had a sense of control over her life. She delighted in the house's subtle sounds—its minor creaks and groans, the cat's paws padding down the stairs, the furnace kicking on and off, and now to be replaced by the air conditioner's automatic cycles.

The first thing Nora wanted to know when she got home was how long it had been before an aide arrived. Julia said, "Oh, not long, maybe 20 minutes or so."

"Was it May?"

"No, Betty came today. She's a nice woman."

"I'm going to call the agency again and stress that it's important that we have someone here on time."

Nora sank into the matching recliner. Sighing, she began to talk about one of her students whose writing skills were so poor that she didn't know how she'd gotten through high school, let alone enrolled in college.

Julia barely heard the details. She just liked watching Nora. Today, she was dressed in a short purple jacket and a long black skirt. She had a paisley scarf swirled around her neck that was purple, black, white, and gray. Julia loved to see her daughter dressed up. She had a sense of style, knew what looked good on herself. Julia had always dressed plainly. Now, she wore stretch polyester pants and tops—cheap and comfortable.

She sent a beam of love toward Nora, and Nora basked in its spotlight for a few minutes.

###

Nora wanted to get a lightweight power chair for her. She had visions of taking Julia with her to Kroger and for short excursions around the neighborhood. She had also investigated activities at the local senior center. Julia, Nora thought, needed friends among her peers. "Mom," she said, "it's not good for you to sit in your recliner so much and depend totally on us for company."

For her part, Julia intended to do just that. Well, she didn't sit *all the time.* She walked up and down the hallway a few times each day, either with her walker or on her own when the nurses' aide came two times each week to check her out and help her with a shower. She faithfully performed some leg flexes and other exercises before she got out of bed each morning, and she had a peddling exerciser that she used while sitting in her recliner. That and her walker were the only mechanical devices she needed.

She was content with the small slice of world she could see from the windows. Though she had never met anyone on the cul-de-sac, except, briefly, one woman who lived next door—and, in fact, hadn't much desire to meet them—she knew their names and their movements. She loved to watch the birds—robins and one blue jay—come to the bath and feeders and the squirrels' antics as they tried to rob the feeders. She could see one feeder from the window facing her recliner. Her son-in-law, John, a kind man, bless him, had hung it there for her.

On her periodic visits to the doctor, Julia was tense and got sick to her stomach. She had grown up in the country and, later, lived in a small town. The motion of the car and the city traffic frightened her and made her dizzy. Nora told

John that Julia was agoraphobic. She'd read that older people sometimes became that way.

One disappointment was not seeing her three great grandchildren enough. They were the children of her only grandson, Don Jr., son of Don, her other child. Now, that she had moved in with Nora and John, the family lived four hours away. There were two twin girls and a boy, three years younger than his sisters—Millie and Mollie, age 10, and a boy, Joe, age 7. The girls were a double blessing, awakening something in her she thought was dead after Susie's death. And little Joe, so cute following his dad around. It was not as though she was active with them; she just liked watching them and listening to them. The coltish girls, giving her shy smiles, then relaxing, bickering with each other and bossing their little brother. Since she'd lived here, she'd seen them only twice on holidays when they made brief visits. Photos and occasional, brief phone chats weren't enough.

###

"Do you know what Mom asked me to buy her today?"

"A scooter?"

"Very amusing. No, she asked for Campbell's Chicken and Stars soup."

"What's the matter with that? Yum-yum. Are we having that for dinner?"

"John–n–n, don't you know it's laden with salt? 500 milligrams of sodium per serving. For God's sake, she takes Lasix—a diuretic. You know, too much salt can make her retain water, lead to congestive heart failure."

"I guess I didn't think of that. Did you tell her that?"

"Yes, I did."

"What did she say?"

"She says she's good most of the time, and she just has a craving."

"Well, I think she has a point."

"Do you think I should cook it for her?"

"Well, it seems to me that, at age 73, you should be able to make some decisions for yourself, even if they're not the wisest. Would one bowl of Chicken & Stars soup hurt her that much?"

"You're a cream puff! I love her, but she's a wily old woman."

###

Julia knew that Nora fancied herself in love with her psychologist. She knew this because she had mentioned him a few too many times. She knew because of the way she said his name, Dr. Evans, with a little catch in her voice and an attempt to sound casual. And she knew just because she knew Nora.

She was also certain that the psychologist was professional and was not taking advantage of Nora's affection for him. Nora was, well, romantic, and cared about *literature*. And there was a part of her that had been broken ever since Susie's death. She'd had no other children to focus on.

Nora was the different one in the family. Her brother Don was a lot like his father, Porter—practical, mechanically talented. He hadn't particularly liked school, though he finished high school and got decent grades. Shortly after graduating, he managed to start a local trucking business and had done well. Education for both Julia and Porter had stopped at the eighth grade, though Julia had studied and gotten her GED and had worked as a nurse's aide for over twenty years.

John, her son-in-law, was a good, practical man, a personnel director for a large company. Julia was certain Nora loved John. She regarded Nora's infatuation with her psychologist as a "This, too, will pass" situation. Honestly! A psychologist was *paid* to listen and be understanding.

She thought about her own marriage. She supposed some people might call it … what was the word she'd heard on Oprah? Dysfunctional. He liked to drink and hang around the pool room with his buddies. He was a good-looking guy, and she knew that he'd been unfaithful to her at least once. She suspected more. But they had stayed together, and they loved each other in their own way.

Once, she'd been tempted herself. One of Porter's friends treated her special and liked to hear her point of view on things—something Porter did less and less the longer they were married. They kissed and "made out," as the kids say. He was married, too. Porter didn't know.

###

Julia woke during the night. *Something wrong—a heaviness. Did she fall asleep reading with her book falling on her chest? No. Now taking deep breaths—gasping. Her heart—what she dreaded. Keep calm. The bell. Where was it? Then, it was in her hand. She was ringing it. It wasn't loud enough.*

"Nora! Nora, I need help! Nora!"

Then Nora was leaning over her, trying not to panic.

"Mom, what's the matter, mom?"

"Can't breathe. Pain in my chest"

"John, call 911! John!"

Nitro under her tongue. Cherry flavored aspirin on top of her tongue. Nora sitting on her bed holding her hand.

151

John rushes in. "They're on the way!"

Then, there were men invading her room. Why were there so many?   Must be six. Checking her pulse. Taking her blood pressure.

Nora explaining about her bypass—congestive heart failure.

They were lifting her and strapping her onto the gurney, wrapping a blanket around her so she'd be warm. Wheeling her past the bird feeder, down the sidewalk, into the ambulance. Sirens, the flashing red light. Everything so fast in this city.

One of the guys patted her head. "How you doin', hon?"

Then, he squeezed and held her hand.

She was in the hospital for a week. They adjusted her medications. They ran tests. They told her that one of the bypasses was partially blocked. They ruled out a balloon angioplasty. They would manage her condition with medication. Then, they sent her to a nursing home—a temporary stay where she would receive round-the-clock care and observation.

Nora hated the nursing home. She didn't say so, but Julia knew.

She would come at night to visit and sit, tense and fidgety, in the bedside chair. The other patient in the room was a whiner, a complainer, who wanted constant attention from the nurses.

Nora drew the curtains between the beds and whispered, "How can you stand that, Mom?"

"I always get crazy roommates, remember. It makes the nurses appreciate me more. I'm the sweet one. . ."

"Oh, Mom," Nora managed to smile.

"Go, Nora. Go home. You have things to do. Papers to grade. I'll be okay. They'll let me out of here in a week or so."

Nora left, trying not to show her relief at being allowed to escape.

###

Julia had the *Today Show* on, but her attention was more focused on the front page of the morning paper. May was sitting on the bed folding laundry.

Then, she sensed the urgency in the voices. She saw the top of one of the World Trade Towers on fire and dropped the paper into her lap.

"Some reports are it was a small commuter plane."

"I didn't get the impression it was that big a plane."

An eyewitness report: "an enormous fireball ... hundreds of dozens of papers flying through the air like confetti ..."

"It was a jet, a very large plane ... might have been a DC9.... Oh, another one just hit!"

"It literally flew itself into the World Trade Center."

"I wonder if there are air traffic control problems."

"Could be a 727 ... at least a 727."

Katie Couric: "This is so shocking!" (But her tone of voice didn't convey shock. She seemed deliberately trying to stay calm.)

"And now you have to move from an accident to something deliberate ..."

Julia and May sat in shock as did the rest of the nation. Julia couldn't remember anything—well, maybe the assassination of JFK—that had left her this dumbstruck.

153

The telephone rang. It was Nora calling from the college. "Oh mom, are you watching TV?"

Julia nodded, and then realized she had to respond in words.

"Yes, Nora, it's awful."

"I'll be right home. Try to be calm."

Julia switched off the TV. *I'll just sit here and be quiet and listen to the house sounds. That'll help me calm down.*

But minutes later, she turned it on again, mesmerized by the awfulness.

When Nora came home from the funeral, she went to Julia's room and sank into the recliner. She thought about how thankful she was for the past four years with her mom—how, before she came to live with them, the doctor had taken her aside telling her "You should realize what you're letting yourself in for. She's going to need a lot of care."

Yes, it had been difficult. The pattern repeated three times over the past several months. Julia would be stable for a while, then there'd be a scary episode. The 911 call. The emergency squad. The hospital stay while they tried to find the right combination of meds. Then, Julia would be back in her room, maybe a little weaker, needing a little more oxygen, a little less active, but still soldiering on. Thank God, she was always lucid, almost cheerful, a little sassy. Then, the final episode just a month after the September 11 attacks.

At the hospital, Nora told a doctor, "I think it was September 11. The shock was too much for her."

The doctor replied, "Well, maybe, but it would have happened soon anyway. She had a very weak heart."

Her heart was getting mechanical support. The doctors said she might not live long without it, and Julia calmly chose to disconnect it. She lasted about four hours after that, lucid until the end. Her last words: "I love you, Nora."

I held my mom while she died How did I do that? It seemed impossible. But it also seemed right—somehow transcendent.

She would do it all again—these last four years.

Then, a memory from long ago fell over her like a shadow. When she was a sophomore in high school, she and Julia were at odds with each other. Julia had smelled smoke on her clothing and accused her of "going wild." She'd said smoking was not "ladylike." Defiantly, Nora scoffed. "I don't want to be a boring old lady. Besides …" She'd nearly asked what Julia knew about being a lady anyway but stopped short.

Julia had been right about the wildness, more than she knew. Nora had skipped afternoon classes to smoke, drink beer, and make out with guys in the back seat of cars. In her junior year, she was saved by Mr. Harvey, her English lit teacher, who turned her on to Shakespeare and told her she should go to college because she had a fine mind. Yes, it was Mr. Harvey and Shakespeare who set her on the right track, not Julia with her lectures.

Finally, Nora stood and went to the spare bedroom that served as her office. She opened the file cabinet and pulled out a poem that she had worked on and revised many times. A poem that made her feel guilty for writing it. A poem that she had discussed only with Dr. Evans, her psychologist. A poem that she would probably never consider "finished." She read the latest version:

HISTORY

A galvanized metal bucket
it must have been
plastic wasn't common then
for household tasks and uses
such as this

a container for organic matter
the mother tended by others
an aunt and who?
a friend or a doctor in the room

the girl should not have entered
the aunt explained to her
it had to be done.
She wasn't sure it belonged to him.

The daughter was 10, 11, or 12.
How could a girl that age
absorb this without spilling over

Keeping a silence beget
by silence, tempted to be
a Pandora of family secrets

The mother lived 74 years, surviving
cardiac failures, bypasses and more.
Her dearness and frailty shields
against intrusive questions.

The devoted keeper
of three fat ceramic pigs
for great grandchildren's futures.

Julia had turned 75 two days before she went to the hospital. Without realizing what she was doing, Nora changed the 74 to 75, and that act triggered her tears. She hadn't been able to cry since Julia died, but now she sobbed—sobbed for the loss of her mother, sobbed for things left unsaid over the years, sobbed until she was exhausted. At the edge of sleep, it came to her that she believed, as she might not fully have believed before, that Julia was entitled to her secrets. ∎

Mr. John Jones

I grew up in a four-room, tin-roofed, brick house in rural Missouri. It had a front porch that stretched the width of the house and an unfinished attic that was drafty in the winter and sweltering in the summer. In the spring and early fall, the attic was a private place for me to play among stacks of boards, boxes of mementos, and odd chairs, tables, and tools for which we no longer had any use. The small, dark basement under the kitchen was lined with makeshift shelves that held jars of green beans, tomatoes, grape jelly, and blackberry jams, the fruits of our summer labors and my mother's canning. Gunnysacks of potatoes grown in our garden took up most of the basement floor space during the winter. Until I was about 12 years old, the house had no indoor plumbing. We used an outhouse, imperfectly hidden by a sizeable pile of bricks, in the far corner of the backyard.

My parents and I occupied three rooms, a kitchen, a bedroom for them, and another room that doubled as a living room and a bedroom for me. I slept on a foldout couch that many nights I failed to fold out. In that room also was a large, black coal stove--our source of heat that I regarded as a necessary, fearsome nuisance. Years later, it occurred to me that the smoke and fumes from the coal may have been the source of my frequent respiratory ailments.

The other room was occupied by Mr. John Jones, the actual owner of the house. My folks had an arrangement. They provided his food and took care of the place in exchange for living there rent-free.

I thought of the house as ours and John—for that's what I usually called him even when I was very young—as our renter. At some point, perhaps at age 8 or 9, I began to want a room of my own. I told my mother I wished John didn't rent a room from us; then, I could have his room. She sat me down and set me straight. I was not ever to say that again! Moreover, I was not to annoy Mr. John Jones in any way. We had a good deal, she said, and he had told my dad that we could have the house when he passed away.

If the house was less than adequate, the grounds offered an abundance of space and natural beauty. The yard was huge with stately oaks and three large pines that yielded cones. The large pasture was rented to neighbors who needed more land for their animals. Near the house, we had a large garden for tomatoes, peas, onions, and such, as well as an orchard with apple trees, and farther away, a long, narrow garden mostly for potatoes, and near that plot, a big blackberry patch. Beyond the pasture was a wooded area where my father and other men hunted rabbits, squirrels, and raccoons. Some fifty acres altogether Mr. John Jones owned and permitted us to live on!

John himself was an eccentric, a man of few words and few social contacts. I thought he might be the dullest man in the world, but he was also something of an enigma and a source of amusement. A thin man of medium height with a long face and pale blue, watery eyes, he was in his early seventies when I first knew him. He always wore faded overalls covered by a faded denim jacket and a hat, even in the heat, for he said the summer winds gave him colds.

John was known throughout the community for "still having the first nickel he ever earned." He was rumored to be worth a great deal of money, but where and how he accumulated it was never clear. Aside from owning the property we lived on, I could see no signs of wealth. He lived and dressed like a pauper, mending his old shirts and overalls until they fell apart.

John structured his days rigidly by the clock. At 2:50 p.m. each day, he rose from the porch swing, or perhaps from an old, wooden rocking chair under the oak in front yard, and walked down our long driveway to the well to slake his thirst. His eyes were usually focused on the ground or on some point out in the field; his legs moved in long methodical strides. When he reached the well behind the garage, the crank would creak and the chain would groan, and everyone knew it was 3 o'clock. The same thing happened daily at 6:10, 9:50, and 11:50 a.m., and at 5:50 and 7:50 p.m., at which time he would fill a jar with water to place by his bed overnight.

John got up at 6 a.m. and went to bed at 9 p.m. He ate his meals at 6:30 a.m., 12:00 noon, and 6 p.m. He chewed tobacco three times a day, mid-morning, mid-afternoon, and midway between supper and bedtime. Our meals were planned around his schedule. If mom had a meal prepared before his scheduled time, he ignored her call and waited until that time to come to the kitchen. When Missouri adopted daylight saving time, John ignored it and fixed his own meals until he and mom reached a tacit compromise. He fixed his own breakfast, she fixed his lunch on his schedule, but he ate dinner with us on daylight saving time.

Despite my mom's lecture, I could not summon much gratitude to John for our living arrangements. Having been warned, I took to more subtle ways of annoying him—actions that could be interpreted as natural childish mischief. He was phobic about being photographed, so when I got a camera one Christmas, I devoted a good deal of time the following spring and summer to sneaking a photo of him. When he caught me, he'd scowl and say, "Get out of here!" His face flushed, and he'd move his chair to a different part of the yard. Only once did I get a photo of him. He was walking down the driveway in midstride. I showed it to him triumphantly, and he harrumphed, making an almost playful grab for it.

I also sat in the porch swing in front of his room with my country & western songbooks and sang until my voice was hoarse. Usually, he ignored me, but a couple of times he came stomping out of his room, saying "That's about enough of that noise."

The one social activity John truly seemed to enjoy was playing a card game called pitch with my grandpa. Weather permitting, he'd walk a mile to my grandparents' house, where I often visited and played with my cousin who lived nearby. When my cousin and I got bored with paper dolls and dress-up, we'd play cards with them. We'd start out serious, but then, goof around, giggling, hiding cards to win, or eating while we played—antics designed to irritate but not to the point that they'd actually banish us from the game. We knew they preferred four-handed pitch to two-handed, and we also knew how to test the limits without exceeding them. "Play cahds!" John would demand of us.

In my teens, of course, I outgrew these childish diversions and became preoccupied with my own insecurities. I had to make the adjustment from attending a one-room country school to a city high school where I felt like a hillbilly.

Later, I was to live in large cities, first in an apartment where I treasured the privacy of my own bedroom, and then in a four-bedroom house in the suburbs with my husband and two children. I became a city person.

John's arrangement with my parents continued in its usual, circumscribed manner for several years. Then, one hot, humid summer day, John walked down the driveway for the last time. He had a heart attack and was found lying near the well, wearing his jacket, of course, with his hat beside him.

Two wills were found, both unwitnessed, written in John's spidery hand on cheap, lined stationery. One left his estate to his next of kin, a niece who'd never visited or corresponded with him, insofar as my parents knew, in all the years they had lived with him. The other left the property to my parents. The matter went to probate, and, after some time, my parents were granted rights to the property, possibly because the magistrate was an acquaintance—a tall, portly man with a booming voice who loved to eat and sometimes attended "coon" suppers held by my dad and his friends to feast on the bounty of their out-of-season hunting. As for the niece, she showed up soon enough to inherit a six-figure bank account, minus some modest probate costs. Thus, it was, those rumors of wealth were finally confirmed, but, these many years later, I still think of John as our "renter." ■

POEMS

Raiment for My Daughter

For Natalie, 1996

My funeral dress was airy black
light and loose and long
falling almost to my ankles
I was spilled ink
flowing on an impermeable surface.

Three days earlier
I wore hospital scrubs
pajamas offered by a kind nurse
my stomach tense as a surgical clamp
in the bed next to yours.

From your wardrobe
I took two items
an oversized flannel shirt
to comfort me in winter's pall

and a dressy blouse
magenta geometry with scrolls,
patches of pink, teal, lavender and gold
to lend me your grace and smile

One left me numb,
the other streamed light
from stained-glass windows
to become a shroud

Last Christmas you modeled
long baggy sweaters
and lean leggings
"I've always wanted to be thin," you said.

Watching you twirl,
I tried to fit the shape, the shadows,
the contours of you into my synapses

An unskilled seamstress
with no pattern
taking fearful measurements.

Connection

Wild Cat Cleo will not be ignored.
She presses her case for freedom--
her nature, not my nurture.

There, the door is open.
Go before I change my mind!

Go out if you must
do whatever cats do
sniff and scratch, stalk and prowl
slip silently into the dark
black on black, camouflaged.

Do what you must do
but come back to me
don't quarrel with the neighbor's
menacing tom, eat bad meat, or run
in front of moving vans.

I must care for you,
Cat Cleo, as your once mistress,
my daughter, did
bury my face in your fur, her hair

Leave the senses of the night
come inside where it's safe and light
bring me your feline mantras,
your small, sad song.

She was kind and gentle,
kind and gentle, kind and gentle.

This we both knew—
and I, much more.

Our Good Wooden Fence

"Good fences make good neighbors."
- *Mending Wall*, by Robert Frost

The cottonwood tree
that towers taller than our house
conspires with the wind
to scatter its autumn leaves
beyond our backyard fence
to our neighbor's well-kept lawn.

I wonder if they grumble
over their evening meal, saying
"We should ask them to rake our yard!"
Our good wooden fence does not suffice.

The knotted rope that holds the gate,
my autistic son cleverly unties
lacking that, there is the door
he slyly unbolts
to visit another deck
where he is not welcome

It reminds him of another
where he sat for hours
transfixed by the dance of leaves
and limbs against the sky
that has no property lines.

Our good wooden fence does not suffice.

For an Autistic Son

For Nathan

Your hand in the crook of my elbow
Your much larger hand in mine.
At first glance, strangers might think

it is you guiding. Then they might notice
that you don't quite look them in the eye
the feet that drag in the gravel

a sort of goofiness, a word
more endearing than clinical terminology
so cool and unconnotative of affection.

Your head a head above my head, sometimes
I look up startled. You, something of a giant
unconquered, schlepping along beside me.

Autism

In a smile's shimmer
I glimpsed sun-tipped waves
coral-covered, sunken treasure.

In a fragment of repose
I saw deep Crater Lake blue
calm formed from volcanoes.

Your eyes make contact
a fleeting connection at dawn
flickering, evaporating, gone.

Darkening in the sky
you do not know you
rain in my eye.

From the periphery
you watch the earth spin
know self-gravity.

Your prospects on earth
may be limited, I'm apprised.
Others miss the universe
I've seen in your eyes.

Plain Thoughts about Things

What will be done with the things?
A nonspecific word to be avoided
in poetry. Connotation of
tangible. Well, usually.
How are things? An exception.

In old age, a question some
may not want to pursue
specifically though others
might be greedy for detail.

My mother's things -
quilts carefully stitched
that matched no one's tastes.
Photos of people I can't identify.
Some still boxed, never viewed.

Our friends' things -
purged for assisted living.
Years of *National Geographic.*
Scientific tomes, evidence
of intellect no library wants.

My own things -
An owl collection, perhaps
destined for eBay. Poetry
and short story collections.
My sons are not literary.

Things evoke pride and pleasure.
Then require ruthlessness.
I lack the guillotine urge
to lop off sentiment. But I vow:

Tomorrow, I will find a home
for my mother's lavender afghan.

Public Dreaming

Scrunched down in a chair
not meant for sleeping
even so, dozing sweetly

with a prolonged wakening
like savoring the last pages
of a novel I don't want to end

A sometime insomniac in my own bed
I have become a public napper
in the afternoon hush

of the public library fiction section
slumbering among discreet readers
too preoccupied or polite to notice

Awake, my eyes slide lazily
over the B's—the brothers
have been shifted again.

Twins, both authors
one better known than the other
I knew in another library long ago.

We were discontented clerks
insufferable I'm sure
"A trained monkey could do this."

He seethed with ambition
to have his own books
pushed across counters.

I was underemployed
prideful of my degrees and
insights into Henry James.

He had red hair and pale blue
go-to-hell eyes behind
round wire-rimmed glasses

The brashness and swagger
of a revolutionary and feigned contrition
if anyone took offense.

I keep meaning to take one of his books
to the circulation desk and push
it across the counter

But I've gotten no further than the
book jacket with his fuller visage
and somewhat satisfied smile

his plots less compelling than his persona—
a developing character in the novel
I'm still planning to write.

Dancers

Picture the pro at the Ohio Star Ball
body straight in tuxedo and perfect pause
the dancer's required smile.

He is the antithesis of all that--
old and bent and bald with a spare
tire above the waist and flat hips lost
in loose, much washed, gray polyester pants.

He prefers one partner
not his wife who stopped dancing
after a stroke some years ago
If she doesn't show, he leaves early

She would prefer a younger, taller
man who doesn't laugh at his own jokes
but they like to talk and she can follow
his interesting, idiosyncratic style

She is prone to exaggerate her dance resume
the partners she had in grander days
but, still, he is surprisingly firm
and confident in his lead.

And they'll keep meeting on Saturday nights
until one doesn't come any more
or until she finds a partner
who is younger and taller.

An Evening at the Symphony

The symphony gushes, swirls and drains
and I am nodding off, my husband
eyeing me surreptitiously,
concerned or embarrassed?

The renowned guest pianist has a substantial
girth, many competitions under his belt
but his hands are not the thin graceful hands
that slowly lifted, curved and hovered,
making breathing secondary

At intermission, I disappear into the crowd
returning at second call to avoid my shrink,
attentive to the woman at his side.
I am jealous of her access.

On the trip home, we are silent
the rain aggressive, intense, troubling
cars slice by in defiance
freeway lights blur and tremble and break
sending their shards heavenward

Is everything all right? he asks.
There is a spin, a crash, a flashing
moment when everything
almost becomes nothing.

But now I am in my bed grateful
for dry insomnia and a rumba *muy triste*
running through my mind
sheepish over my sulk

because I'd wanted to go dancing instead.

Landscaping Scenes from a Marriage

The woebegone Boston fern
I unceremoniously dumped
in the woods near our backyard

my husband rescued with an injured
air and hung in a place of honor
on a limb of the decorative apple tree.

Now in its second season the fern still
mostly a matted tangle of roots and straw
mocks me with its few tenacious fronds.

The Canadian hemlock failed to thrive
more brown than green last year, a scrawny
specimen among five vigorous peers

I suggested a warranty replacement.
"Give it time," he replied, and I thought
"Oh, do we have to go through this again?"

This spring the tree is a gangly adolescent
challenging nature with a layer of lush new
growth, accusing me of shortsightedness.

The blue spruce has a different history.
Bred for special service, a living Christmas
tree. We took it from its element, bestowed

it with our glitter, celebrated it yet burdened it,
exploited it, not noticing as its needles dried
and shriveled. Were we guilty of neglect?

Then, we thrust it back into the cold, familiar
earth where it struggled under our common
watch, finally becoming a tree for more seasons...

Smiley's People: Précis & Appreciation

From Paris, a Russian émigré wrote to the imposing
General, unknowingly giving him information
he'd awaited for years: She'd been approached by
a Russian thug talking of the daughter she deserted
long ago. A legend for a girl! the General declared.
He sent Leipzig, the magician, with the dancing eyes.

And called Smiley, England's legendary MI6 spy,
who found both men dead, chalk marks their bequest.
Moscow Rules, of course. Torture most monstrous:
Karla's way – his ruthlessness and weakness
exposed, a beloved daughter who must have a legend,
a heritage, not his own, to leave Mother Russia.

And, thus, the wheels were set in motion for Smiley
the modest spy who received respectful glances
from all who'd worked with him or heard about him.
His only weakness: Ann, beloved wife who cuckolded
him many times, unforgivingly (perhaps) even
with bloody Bill Hayden, Karla-run, Circus traitor.

East versus West, allegiances and betrayals
Oh, what parallels, LeCarre! two master spies –
adversaries for years. Which one would triumph?
I knew very well – having read the novel possibly
six times. This time while feeling blue after some
successes and understanding Smiley perfectly

when he (almost) regretted Karla walking across
the Berlin bridge to him and his people – wishing
(almost) Karla's people would shoot from the tower.
Not even thoughts of Ann in Bill's arms allowing
him to fully revel. Guillam says, "George, you won."
His reply: "Did I? "Yes. Yes, well I suppose I did."

Silence and Smoke

An only child, secretive by nature
I would rise on sleepless summer nights

feeling my way like an intruder
and from our unlit kitchen see

the then comforting orange glow
as he sat under the tall oak tree

his smoke borne by indifferent breezes
into the darkness. For me the scent

of mystery and masculinity.
What did he think about on those evenings?

That I never figured out. My father,
a Missouri country man of few words.

No need to talk when he could smoke
or cough and wheeze and spit

on winter mornings and evenings
less idyllic long before the final silence.

Pronouns

They folded you up and crated you.

They will never let you write a novel.
Or if they did, they'd never let it be published.

They park outside your apartment, read your email,
listen to your telephone conversations.

Once, you tried to make a friend. They called
and warned him you're not a worthy person.

They are the alien it – origin unidentified –
chemistry, faulty circuits, or genetic defects.

They are it and it is you, though not the true you
and you don't know it is you, and neither you

nor anyone else is to blame for the way
you have folded and crated your life.

About The Author

Barbara Kussow's fiction often includes characters who are in middle age or old age. For ten years, she edited and published a literary magazine titled *Still Crazy* that published short stories, essays, and poetry written by or about people over age 50. She wrote about the magazine in an essay for *Writing After Retirement* (Rowman & Littlefield, 2014; ed. Carol Smallwood & Christine Redman-Waldeyer),

Kussow is the author of a novel entitled *Portrait of Annie* and a novella, *An Abolitionist Family; a Tale of the Civil War Era.* Short fiction and poetry published in online and paper venues are included in this collection

Publishing Notes

Stories were previously published as follows:

"The Vigilante," "A Sunday Afternoon," "Mr. John Jones," and "Apple Blossoms" in different issues of *The Storyteller.*

Chapter Six of "The Merlin Subsidiary" was adapted from "Learning to Dance," in *Wild Violet,* September 2, 2012.

"1984" in *Wild Violet,* June 23, 2013.

"After Class" in *Mysterical-e,* an online magazine.

Poetry was previously published as follows:

"Autism" in *Psychological Poems, J. of Outsider Poetry,* October 2011, with a different title.

"Connection" in *Wild Violet,* October 7, 2013.

"For an Autistic Son" in *The Dos Passos Review,* Spring 2009.

"Landscaping Scenes from a Marriage," *Main Channel Voices* (now defunct), Spring 2009.

"Our Good Wooden Fence," *Kaleidoscope,* Summer/Fall, 2005.

"Plain Thoughts about Things, *Months-to-Years,* an online zine, 2018."

"Public Dreaming," *ByLine* (now defunct), February 2007.

(continued)

"Raiment for my Daughter," *Byline* (now defunct), (Honorable Mention in contest); *Red Owl* (now defunct).

"Silence and Smoke" in *Hospital Drive,* the journal of the University of Virginia School of Medicine, *July 9, 2013.*

Other poetry was published by *Danse Macabre*, an online magazine.